Malabarista

FOR MORE ON THESE AND OTHER TITLES,
VISIT WWW.NEWESTPRESS.COM

Garry Ryan

MALABARISTA

A Detective Lane Mystery

NeWest Press

COPYRIGHT © GARRY RYAN 2011

LIBRARY AND ARCHIVES CANADA CATALOGUING IN PUBLICATION

Ryan, Garry, 1953–
Malabarista : a detective Lane mystery / Garry Ryan.

ISBN 978-1-897126-89-9

I. Title.

PS8635.Y354M35 2011   C813'.6   C2011-901968-X

Editor for the Board: Doug Barbour
Cover and interior design: Natalie Olsen, Kisscut Design
Author photo: Karma Ryan
Copyediting: NJ Brown and Paul Matwychuk

 Canada Council for the Arts Conseil des Arts du Canada   Canadian Heritage Patrimoine canadien

 accessCOPYRIGHT FOUNDATION   edmonton **arts** council   Alberta **Foundation** for the Arts

NeWest Press acknowledges the support of the Canada Council for the Arts, the Alberta Foundation for the Arts, and the Edmonton Arts Council for our publishing program. We acknowledge the financial support of the Government of Canada through the Canada Book Fund for our publishing activities.

NeWest Press #201, 8540–109 Street
Edmonton, Alberta T6G 1E6
780.432.9427
www.newestpress.com

No bison were harmed in the making of this book.

printed and bound in Canada   1 2 3 4 5 13 12 11

FOR JIM

AND MARYANNE

Ordinary riches can be stolen from a man. Real riches cannot. In the treasury-house of your soul, there are infinitely precious things, that cannot be taken from you.

OSCAR WILDE,
"The Soul of Man Under Socialism"

chapter 1

"This is the only way the two of you can stay in touch. Glenn passes Cam's message to me, and I pass it on to you. Since Cam's the one heading up the investigation into the charges against you, he has to keep his distance until it's done." Matt pulled on the leash, as Roz, their Australian cattle dog, dragged him along on their walk.

Lane had to move quickly to keep up to Matt, who appeared to be about to fall after each awkward step. They turned off the sidewalk and down a trail just wide enough for them to travel single file. Matt bent to let Roz off the leash. She lunged ahead.

The air was cooler in the shadow of the trees. Lane grabbed a mosquito out of the air and crushed it in his fist.

"Do you miss Harper?" Matt stopped in a clearing to sit on a toppled tree trunk. He rubbed his beard: a first attempt. It was black, the same shade as what was left of the hair on his Uncle Arthur's head.

Lane sat down next to him. "Yes."

"Glenn said that his uncle is pissed about Chief Smoke demanding an investigation of the lost Glock, but can't do anything about it. Yet. Glenn told me to make sure I remembered to say 'yet' with lots of irony. And he wanted you to know that Smoke is trying to do a number on both of you after your last case embarrassed him. Smoke wants Harper to look like he's turning on his old partner." Matt turned to study his uncle's reaction.

McTavish warned me to watch my back, Lane thought.

"He also said that Harper will do the investigation by the book," Matt said.

Of course, Lane thought as he looked down the trail. Roz came galloping back to see what was holding them up. *You can trust Cam Harper. You trusted him with your life. Being investigated could turn out to be a stroke of luck, if you can survive all of the crap in between.* "Leaving the Glock behind was a show of faith."

"What do you mean?" Matt asked.

"We all put our guns down as a show of faith. We were all putting our weapons into a pile to be destroyed. It was the only way to put an end to the killings." Lane watched as Roz backed up with her tail tucked under her belly. She sat between them and looked back the way she'd come.

"Do you think Uncle Arthur's biopsy will be okay?" Matt asked.

Lane looked at his nephew and saw the worry in the lines across his forehead. Lane tried to smile but found he couldn't. *How do I explain this nagging sense of foreboding?*

They heard the bark of another dog as it crashed into the clearing. The black fur at the back of its neck stood up like it was gelled. The dog was at least twice the size of Roz. Its head was low with its muzzle brushing the ground as it glared at her.

"Back off!" Matt said.

"She's friendly." A man entered the clearing. He was dressed for golf. His grey hair was cut close and his face was clean-shaven. The dog's leash was looped around his neck. "Isn't that right, Chief?"

Chief moved closer to Roz and growled. Lane grabbed Roz's collar. "Put Chief on his leash."

"Chief's friendly." The dog's owner sounded offended.

Chief moved closer. He growled and bared his teeth. Roz backed up. Chief lunged, snarling and snapping at Roz's throat and Lane and Matt's knees. Roz dodged left, tearing away from Lane. The dogs stood growling and spitting as they raised themselves onto their hind legs. Roz lunged. One of the dogs whimpered. Chief was on his back. Roz stood on his chest and bared her teeth.

"Call your dog off!" the man said.

Matt moved forward, grabbed Roz's collar, and pulled her back to the log. The man hooked the leash into Chief's collar. "You gotta watch your dog. He's dangerous."

"She," Lane said.

"What?" The man backed down the path.

"Our dog is a she."

"Better learn to control her better." The man walked back the way he'd come.

Matt looked at his uncle. "But Chief came after Roz."

Lane rubbed Roz behind the ears. "It's funny how the aggressor acts after getting the worst of the fight."

chapter 2

"Detective Lane, you're responsible." Staff Sergeant Gregory delivered the assignment as an edict.

The order was delivered from above, Lane thought. It was well-known that Gregory was a member of the Scotch drinkers' club, a network of "elite" officers who gathered once a month with like-minded citizens to drink Scotch and advance their careers.

Gregory sat at the head of the conference table. His freshly shaved head shone and his neck was red, either from sunburn or a tight collar. "Get on it. The Forensics Unit is at the scene." His manicured fingers propelled the file across the tabletop to Lane, who sat apart from the other detectives. Gregory shared a smile with the other detectives, implying a private joke. "You're dismissed."

Lane looked up from the file to the faces of his colleagues. One looked at the door. Another developed an interest in his fingernails. A third smiled at Gregory and nodded at the joke.

Lane saw his face reflected in the glass wall. He saw the close-cropped black hair with a hint of grey here and there, the missing earlobe, and the blue eyes. *It's as if I'm seeing someone else across the table. I've lost weight.*

"See you later, princess," Gregory said.

Lane picked up the file, stood up, pushed his chair back in, walked to the door, opened it, and stepped outside. *Take your time. Close it very, very softly. It's amazing how quickly word got around that I was under investigation.*

Twenty minutes later, he was driving north out of downtown, up out of the river valley, and passing the outlet shops downwind from the city dump. Lane tried to concentrate on the case at hand. At a stoplight, he glanced at the map on the passenger seat. *A month ago, Harper would have been driving and I would have been giving directions.*

He turned west. The Chev hummed, finally free to stretch out along a straight, two-lane section of highway.

Another turn south and he found the Forensics Unit, a mobile landmark with its blue-and-white paint scheme, parked just off the pavement. Yellow tape encircled the ditch and nearby slough. Inside the barrier, the cattails and grass grew waist-high. The slough had evaporated after a month-long dry spell, leaving a surface of white soil etched with cracks. Here and there were muddy indentations where one of the forensic investigators in their white bunny suits had broken through the surface to expose the mud underneath.

The remains were situated close to the south end of the slough, within ten metres of the road. Dr. Colin Weaver — or Fibre, as he was nicknamed — knelt beside them, his white hood and gauze mask hiding his expression. *Not that there would be one.*

Weaver rocked back on the mud-caked heals of his rubber boots and stood. He turned to one of his white-suited assistants and said, "When you remove the remains, don't worry if you get some of the soil." He held up a bag. "I'll take this in." Fibre turned his face, as handsome as that of a Hollywood celebrity, toward Lane while his assistants laid the body bag next to the remains.

I wonder how Fibre will react to my new circumstances?

Fibre stepped cautiously over the cracked surface of the slough bottom, testing to see if it would support his six-foot frame. He pulled his mask down to his throat as he reached the cattails at the edge of the slough. He held up the bag. "I believe it's a metal case. I cracked it open. It looks like there may be identification inside."

"What was holding the body down?" Lane asked.

Fibre looked over his shoulder. "Two cinder blocks. One chained to the torso, the other to the knees. If it weren't for this dry summer, we might never have discovered it."

"How long has it been there?" Lane asked.

Fibre shook his head and looked in the direction of the mountains, the grey peaks distorted in the haze. "From the state of decomposition, close to a year. You understand that is a very rough estimate?"

Lane nodded.

Fibre pulled back the hood of his bunny suit. Perspiration made his blond hair stick to his scalp and forehead. He held up the bag. "Drive me back to the Foothills Medical Centre and we'll see what's inside of this container."

Lane waited at the Chev as Fibre changed out of his bunny suit and rubber boots. The detective watched the two assistants as they severed the chains with bolt-cutters and painstakingly gathered the remains. Lane could see that a jacket held most of the torso together.

Fibre opened the passenger's door and took a seat. Lane pulled the keys out of his pocket and got in the driver's side. He pulled the seat belt over his shoulder.

"Smoke's motives are transparent. You'll be exonerated," Fibre said.

Lane turned to face the doctor. Fibre's expression was non-committal. *When did you become my friend?* Lane wondered.

Fibre turned to look south at a stand of trees. "It's the time in between being accused and being exonerated that's difficult."

Lane inhaled. The stench of decomposition and slough mud filled the interior of the Chev. "The problem is, some of the mud always sticks."

Fibre shook his head. "Each case is different. An objective analysis of the situation reveals that any type of emotional reaction will cloud your judgment."

Colin, is this still part of your self-imposed penance for what you said to Christine? Lane started the car, shoulder-checked, and accelerated.

"I want to apologize again for what I said to your niece," Fibre said.

Lane held up his hand. Fresh anger lit him from within. He glared at Fibre, who looked down the road.

"I had no right to say that. I understand you've taken in a niece and a nephew. That you and your partner are raising them. That you are very protective of children in general and these two specifically. That is why what I said was particularly odious." Fibre's right knee was dancing up and down as he spoke.

Lane shook his head. *Who would believe this? Fibre running off at the mouth to me. And he's been doing some digging into my background.*

Fibre held up the bag. "I got a glimpse of the ID. It's protected with a clear plastic laminate. I should have some answers relatively quickly. You can accompany me into the lab if you like."

No thanks. "I don't like labs. You're the expert." *I won't be able to get the stink out of my skin for weeks.*

Lane gave the doctor his cell number before dropping Fibre off at his office on the northern end of the Foothills Medical Centre. Then he drove down the hill into the river valley for a cup of coffee and some lunch. He found a place to park west of the café and walked back, past the ice cream shop and across the cul-de-sac overfilled with parked cars.

Inside the café, he ordered a mochaccino and a sandwich before finding a table near the window. As he waited, he observed the people chatting in public privacy. He'd consumed half the sandwich and more than half the coffee when his cellphone rang.

"Dr. Weaver?" Lane asked.

"Correct. I have names for you. Do you want them over the phone?"

Lane looked around him. "Want me to bring you a coffee or a sandwich?"

"Not necessary."

Lane heard uncommon emotion in Fibre's reply. The detective looked at the remains of his lunch. "I'll be there in fifteen minutes."

"Good." Fibre hung up.

Fibre was waiting at his desk in an office so sterile it seemed the air was sanitized. Despite the sunshine streaming through the windows, Lane couldn't see a single speck of lint or dust in the air.

Lane set a paper bag down on the desk. Fibre pulled it toward him and opened it. "Nanaimo bar!" He smiled, and nodded for Lane to sit.

"We have several forms of identification. The small metal case provided added protection against decomposition for the plastic licence and another piece of identification that was, fortunately for us, laminated. Here's the driver's licence." Fibre slid a photocopy toward Lane. "And we have this." He slid a second photocopy next to the first.

Both photocopies showed the face of the same man. Similar weight, same height. The second card used the Cyrillic alphabet. The man wore a military uniform and what appeared to be an officer's cap.

"The driver's license says he's Andelko Branimir," Fibre said. "And it gives a local address. The other ID says he's Borislav Goran."

"You can read this one?" Lane pointed at the photocopy with the Cyrillic letters.

Fibre blushed. "I learn languages. It's a hobby of mine." He pointed at the military ID. "It appears the victim served in a paramilitary unit."

"War crimes?" Lane's mind worked to understand the implications.

"Too little information to reach any conclusions as of yet. But yes, I've done a preliminary check, and this unit was implicated in various war crimes." Fibre opened a desk drawer. He pulled out a large manila envelope and slid the photocopies inside.

"Anything else inside the metal case?" Lane asked.

"Pulp. Whatever else was in there was reduced to pulp." Fibre handed the photocopies to Lane. "After the clothing and remains have been analyzed, you'll get a comprehensive report."

Lane stood up to leave. Fibre touched the paper bag. "Thank you. Nanaimo bars are — "

"Decadent," Lane said.

×

"Deputy Chief Simpson wants to see you. He's in charge until Chief Smoke gets back. The appointment is at eight o'clock tomorrow morning." Lori smiled at him from behind her desk. She was blonde, somewhere between forty and fifty, had three kids of her own, and treated the detectives like they were part of her extended family.

Tomorrow I get fired or suspended, Lane thought. *It's just like Smoke to delegate his dirty work to the second in command. And I feel nothing. No disappointment, nothing.*

Lori stood and waved for Lane to follow her into the storage room where the photocopy machine was. "Come into my office."

Lane stepped inside. Lori looked up at him. "I'm not telling you this, but something is up."

Lane waited. *I wonder how much pension I'll get?*

"Things are hopping in the deputy chief's office. A couple of members of the police commission have been in to see him.

Harper's been in there too." Lori leaned right to see if anyone else was nearby.

"Any idea what it all means?" Lane asked.

Lori shook her head. "All I know is that the deputy's secretary has been fielding calls all morning. Way more traffic than usual. All of them from bigwigs. She's even had calls coming in from the States."

Lane shrugged. "And the deputy chief wants to see me?"

"That's right." Lori's phone rang. She pushed past Lane to answer it.

Lane walked toward his office. "Lane?" He turned. Lori was holding the phone against her breast. "I checked on Andelko Branimir for you. It looks like his family still lives in town. And I could find nothing on file for a missing person named Branimir or Goran."

"How can he not have been reported missing?" Lane asked.

Lori shook her head. "Don't know. And. . ." she hesitated. ". . .how's Arthur?"

Lane shrugged. "We're waiting to find out."

×

Fashionably late. That's what his sister-in-law would call it. A busy schedule is essential. As a result, arriving late is, well, expected of one. Being on time would be a social faux pas. Lane looked around the inside of a restaurant he hadn't visited for nearly a quarter of a century. Hardwood, leather upholstery, waiters and waitresses dressed in black and white, and stained glass windows that prevented passersby from seeing inside. He didn't need to look at the menu to know it would hold all manner of steak and potato entrées. Instead, he added cream and sugar to his coffee and waited.

He felt a hand on his shoulder and a kiss on his cheek. "So good to see you." The scent of Margaret's perfume was almost as overpowering as the artificial sweetness in her voice.

Lane felt his appetite disappear.

"Good to see you." Joseph stood above Lane and to his right. He offered a smile and his hand.

Lane fumbled with his napkin as he rose. He stood, blue eyes to blue eyes, with his brother as they shook hands. Joseph tried to crush Lane's fingers but found he could not.

Joseph released his brother's hand and went to pull out the chair for his wife. Lane watched the lunch patrons studying Margaret and Joseph Lane. It was obvious that everyone knew they moved in the most exclusive of social circles. Joseph adjusted his tie and hung his pinstriped navy blue jacket on the back of the chair before he sat. He ran his hand over the shine of his hairless scalp.

"So sorry we're late. This is such a busy time for us. The meeting with the theatre council went long, and Joseph is working with a client on a merger." Margaret's voice was just loud enough to carry to the next four or five tables.

She really needs everyone to hear what's going on in her life. He looked at her strawberry blonde hair and bronzed skin. "Nice tan."

"Thank you." Margaret glanced at Joseph. "We're planning to winter in Phoenix, so I'll be able to stay tanned year round."

Keep talking at that volume, and even the people on the sidewalk will know your plans.

Joseph waved at the waitress hovering nearby, then looked at Lane. "Have you ordered?"

The waitress stood next to Margaret and smiled. "Are you ready to order, Mrs. Lane?"

Neither Margaret nor Joseph looked at the menu. Joseph nodded at Margaret. "I'll have the veal," Margaret said, then leaned back so the waitress could take the menu.

"Prime rib. Medium well. Baked potato." Joseph looked across the table at his brother.

Lane reached for his menu and looked over the salads.

"Greek salad, please." He handed his menu to the waitress.

"Very good. And to drink?" the waitress asked.

Margaret said, "I think a bottle of your best white would be nice."

"I'll stick with the coffee," Lane said.

"Not going to join us in a glass of wine?" Margaret asked as the waitress left.

Lane heard the condescending tone and thought, *To hell with you!* "No."

"We've been thinking about Dad's will," Joseph said.

Thanks for getting right to the point.

"Although you're not mentioned in the will, we. . ." Joseph smiled at Margaret. ". . .would like to make provisions for Christine's education."

Margaret said, "She is part of the family, after all."

"We think the amount we've set aside is quite generous," Joseph said.

The waitress freshened Lane's coffee. A waiter showed Margaret the label on the bottle of wine. With her nod of approval, the waiter uncorked the bottle. He poured a taste into Margaret's glass. Mrs. Lane took a sip, smiled, and accepted more.

Lane added a touch of sugar and cream to his coffee. He stirred and sipped. *The coffee is remarkably good.* Lane put his cup down. "We have a nephew as well." Lane looked at Margaret.

She blessed Lane with a patronizing smile, then nodded at Joseph who was apparently the one to deal with any and all unpleasantries.

"We have no legal obligation to him," Joseph said. "Besides, your relationship with your *boyfriend* does not obligate us in any way to look after *his* nephew."

When Lane had time to think back, he realized it was the way his brother said the word "boyfriend"—the condescending, dismissive tone with which Joseph summed up his relationship with Arthur — that triggered what happened next.

Lane focused on the coffee for a moment. "Arthur and I are, in reality, the parents of two teenagers." He took a breath to restore a measure of calm to his voice, but it did nothing to quell the anger. "We have a responsibility to consider both Christine and Matt. To act in their best interests. Christine is my blood relative. Matt is Arthur's. They're our family — *my* family — and you dismiss them as if they're of no consequence!"

Margaret sniffed, which Lane interpreted as a gesture of divine arrogance. "Well," she said, "I'm sure everyone in this room has a different notion from yours when it comes to defining family."

"Actually, the sarcasm isn't appreciated." Lane pushed his chair back and stood. He pulled a fifty out of his pocket and tucked it under his coffee cup. He pushed his chair in and walked away.

"There is really no need to make a scene!" Margaret said. "Your mother always said you were overly emotional. If memory serves, she even made some comment about your right to exist. You see, I was your mother's confidante."

Lane stopped. He walked back to the table, leaned forward, and looked at his brother. "Arthur and I have two children. Let's see how high the legal fees will run when I contest the will." He glanced left and watched Margaret's tanned face blanch to the colour of a skinned almond. "And I'm sure the media will love to hear all about the way the wayward, overly emotional Lane boy has tarnished the family name and is being cut out of the family fortune."

He walked away, ignoring Margaret calling after him: "There is no reason for you to leave like this!"

×

"How was lunch?" Lori asked as Lane stepped into the office and stood across from her reception desk.

"The coffee was good," he said.

"Don't kid a kidder." She leaned her elbows on her desk.

"I walked out on the condescending bastards!" He sat down in a chair next to the wall.

She reached down into her desk drawer and pulled out a jar of pistachios. "Snack on these."

As he reached for a handful of nuts, he thought, *You're the one good thing about having to spend so much time back in the office. If everybody had a mother like you, homicide detectives would be unemployed.*

"How are the kids?" Lori split open a pistachio shell with her front teeth, dropped the nut into her palm, and popped it into her mouth.

"Matt's going to university, and Christine is going to college." *If I'd kept my big mouth shut, at least one of them would be paid for.*

"I checked out the location of Andelko Branimir. It wasn't as easy as I first thought it would be. Looks like the family has moved. I've got a new address for you. So far, nothing on Borislav Goran. I'll keep digging." She pointed a finger at Lane. "Try a couple of hours on the sites — the ones I emailed to you — and see what you can find. It'll get your mind off the other stuff. Take these with you." She handed him the jar of nuts.

Staff Sergeant Gregory opened the door to his office. His shiny scalp was backlit by the morning sun. He smiled at Lori and glared at Lane. "So the case is already solved?"

Lane turned to walk to his office. He heard Gregory ask, "So what's new, Lori?"

Lori laughed, "A recent study proves that impotence is more prevalent in men who shave their heads!"

Lane looked over his shoulder and caught a glimpse of

Gregory turning red and laughing too loudly before he ducked back into his office and closed the door.

×

Lane parked across the street from the condo with the single-car garage and the number 342 next to its front door. The doorframe was an inoffensive shade of grey and the siding a non-confrontational shade of grey. The trees in the back-yards next to the Chev were staked evergreens. Each back deck had room for a barbecue and a single chair. The stripes of sod were different shades of green, some separating from the next where more water was required. A sprinkler head popped up and sprayed the passenger side of the Chev as his phone rang. Lane reached into his pocket and flipped his cell open. "Hello?"

"Dr. Weaver here. Initial indications are that the victim was hit from behind on the right side of the head. There are fractures to the parietal and occipital bones and a depression in the skull. I'll update you when we have more."

"Thanks," Lane said as Fibre hung up.

Fifteen minutes later, Lane spotted a vehicle in his side mirror: a white subcompact with two women sitting in the front and the words JELENA'S ALTERATIONS printed and underlined in red on the side. Lane looked left. The garage door to unit 342 opened and the white car eased through the opening. As the door closed, Lane saw the driver lift her head and study him in the rear-view mirror.

Lane watched the house for a minute, deciding what he would say and how he would say it. He opened the car door. He was struck by the absence of birdsong; the only noise was the hum of city traffic and the hiss of sprinklers. Lane crossed the street, climbed two steps, and rang the doorbell. He waited a minute, then rang again.

The door opened, revealing a blonde-haired woman who

could have been anywhere between thirty-five and sixty-five. Lane thought, *You were quite beautiful at one time, but that's past.* "Detective Lane. May I come in?"

"Identification?" She pronounced the word carefully with very little evidence of an accent. Lane estimated her weight to be maybe one hundred and twenty pounds. He reached into his inside jacket pocket, opened his ID, and waited while she inspected it.

She turned and walked down the hallway. "Come in."

Lane tucked away his ID. "You're Jelena Branimir?"

"Yelena. It's pronounced Yelena."

Lane spotted Jelena's daughter sitting on the couch. She wore black to match her eyeshadow and hair. Lane nodded. "Then you're Zarafeta?"

"Zacki," she said before pulling a pair of headphones over her studded ears. She adjusted the player in her hand.

Jelena went to the kitchen sink. "Coffee?"

"Yes please." He watched her fill the machine with water and coffee. "A body was discovered. The driver's licence suggests the victim is Andelko Branimir."

Jelena froze. She reached down to support her legs as she fell back into a kitchen chair.

"Jelena?" Lane moved closer to the woman, who held her head in her hands. Zacki, meanwhile, had closed her eyes and leaned back her head. She hummed a song Lane didn't recognize.

"Do you want me to pour you a cup of coffee?" Lane asked Jelena.

Jelena nodded. "Please."

"What do you take in it?"

"Black." She looked out the back window at the trees.

She's seeing something a long way away.

Lane searched out two cups, found milk in the fridge, and waited for a minute before pouring two coffees. Jelena took two sips. "We had a fight. He said he was going back home and then he left."

"How long ago was this?" Lane asked.

"Last fall. Never heard from him again." Jelena cradled the cup in her hands while staring out the window.

Lane looked to his right at Zacki, who had turned up her music. He could hear the singer repeating the word "nightmare" over and over again.

×

Lane's phone rang as he headed south and away from the posh golf and country club across the road from Jelena's condo complex. A Cadillac roared past him, almost drowning out Lori's tearful voice. "Lane? Arthur needs to talk with you."

"What about?" Lane said.

"Call Arthur." Lori hung up.

Lane dialed his home number with the thumb of his right hand. "Arthur?"

"Dr. Keeler phoned," said Arthur. "I've got breast cancer."

It took Lane less than twenty minutes to get home. He found Arthur, Matt, and Christine waiting in the front room, Christine next to Arthur on the couch, Matt across from them in the armchair, staring at the floor. Christine looked up at Lane. "Good, you're here — it's about time."

Lane turned to Arthur. "What did the doctor say?"

Christine pushed her hands back through her black curly hair. "Keeler said that Uncle Arthur has breast cancer, and he sent the information to a surgeon at the Foothills Medical Centre."

"That's it?" Lane felt numb from the shock of the news and frustrated with his inability to concentrate. He sat down.

"We should expect a call from the surgeon." Matt looked up briefly, then went back to staring at the floor.

"What do we do in the meantime?" Christine asked.

Arthur blew his nose and wiped his eyes. "Keeler said the cancer is still small but aggressive. It looks like it was caught early."

Lane looked at Matt. He lifted his head. Matt was trying to say something with his eyes. Roz went over and poked Matt's knee with her nose. Lane couldn't read what Matt was trying to communicate. "What else?"

"All you do is sleep and work." Matt rubbed Roz under her chin.

"When you're not sleeping or working, you just sit and stare at the TV." Arthur leaned forward to put his hands on his knees.

Lane tried to smile. "Is this an intervention?"

"Got a problem with that?" Christine asked.

Lane leaned back in the rocking chair. *What is going on here?*

"Ever since you and Harper saved those two girls, Harper got transferred, and they made you spend more time in the office, you've been like this. Even when we went for a holiday in Vancouver, we had to drag you out of the hotel room to go down to the ocean or out for dinner." Matt sat up straight. Roz went to the kitchen and whined at the back door. Lane got up to let the dog outside.

Matt stood. "Sit down. I'll let her out."

Arthur put his open hand to his chest, just below his throat, and tapped. "We think you're depressed."

Matt came back into the room and sat down.

"I phoned Loraine today," Christine said, "and she said you've got the symptoms of depression. You sleep too much, eat too little, have no interest in the things you used to like to do, and Arthur says you haven't had sex for over a month!" She rubbed Arthur's back.

"Ewwwww — we didn't need to know that!" Matt said.

"I've made an appointment for you to see Dr. Keeler," Arthur said.

"Why are you doing this now?" Lane asked.

"Isn't it obvious?" Christine asked.

"No," said Lane.

Matt said, "You know what Uncle Arthur's like. He wants to know that we'll be taken care of."

Lane found it difficult to breathe.

The phone rang. For an instant they were frozen.

It rang again.

Lane stood and picked it up. "Hello."

"This is Anne from Dr. Dugay's office. Are you Arthur Mereli?"

Lane had to listen carefully to decipher Anne's heavy Scottish accent. "No, I'm his partner, Lane."

"I see. Is Mr. Mereli there?"

Lane looked at Arthur, who was shaking his head and wiping his eyes. "He's here, but it'll be difficult for him to carry on a conversation."

"Could I speak with him for a moment just to verify that I can ask you the questions, then?"

Lane handed the phone to Arthur, who listened and said, "Yes." He handed the phone back to Lane.

"Mr. Lane, do you have a pen and paper handy?" Anne asked.

Lane snapped his fingers and made a writing motion with his right hand. "It's on its way. What kind of cancer are we dealing with?"

"At the moment it's in situ," said Anne.

"In situ?" Lane asked.

"It hasn't moved out of its bubble. Indications are that it may not have spread. Dr. Dugay will be able to tell you more when you come for your appointment."

Christine set pencil and paper on the coffee table in front of Lane. He nodded and mouthed a thank-you. He wrote down Anne's name and the surgeon's. "What's your last name and phone number, please?"

Anne gave it to him along with the address of the surgeon's office.

"The surgeon, is he any good?" Lane asked.

"The very best," Anne said.

Lane waited.

"Could I have your cell phone number and email?" Anne asked.

Lane gave her his cell number and Lori's at work. "She knows how to get a hold of me, even when no one else can."

"Your appointment is a week from tomorrow at three o'clock." She gave Lane detailed directions and advice on where to park.

It's right next door to Fibre's office, he thought.

"Any other questions?" Anne asked.

"What do I tell Arthur?" Lane asked.

"That Dr. Dugay is well-respected. That your family doctor insisted that Arthur be taken in right away. That we'll see the two of you a week from tomorrow at three."

"Thank you," Lane said.

Anne hung up.

Lane looked at the three pairs of eyes waiting to hear the news, so he repeated Anne's message word for word.

chapter 3

Lane looked at his watch. *Seven o'clock on the dot. I need a coffee.*

He leaned against the wall about three metres from Dr. Keeler's office door. *He said to be here no later than seven. It's locked; maybe I've got time to go to Fourth Street and pick up a mochaccino.*

A key rattled on the other side of the lock. The door opened, and the doctor's massive head, with its black eyebrows, heavily lined forehead, broad nose, and white hair, appeared. "There you are!"

Keeler held the door open as Lane walked in, then locked it behind them. He grabbed a file from the counter and waved for Lane to follow him to an examination room. "We'll get you weighed first."

After Lane weighed in, Keeler took his blood pressure. "How's Arthur?" the doctor asked.

"In a state of shock like the rest of us."

"How are you sleeping?"

"That's about all I do. Sleep and work." Lane felt the squeeze of the expanding blood pressure band on his arm.

"How about your appetite?" Keeler put his stethoscope on the inside of Lane's elbow.

What appetite?

Keeler peeled off the armband. "Well?"

Lane shrugged. "Food tastes like paste."

"Look." Keeler checked Lane's fingernails then watched his eyes. "We both know why you're here. Arthur phoned Mavis because he's worried about you, and she got you in first thing this morning."

Lane nodded.

"Arthur thinks you're depressed. By the look of you and the amount of weight you've lost, I tend to agree. Have you been thinking about suicide?"

Lane shrugged.

"I want you to see a psychiatrist, and I'd like to prescribe medication." Keeler wrote Lane a prescription. "Take one a day. After three weeks, see me again, and we'll see if it's necessary to up the dosage."

Lane took the prescription.

"Will you see a psychiatrist or psychologist? I can recommend a couple." Keeler crossed his arms.

"What do you think?" Lane asked.

"Arthur gave us a name he got from a friend of yours. She's a very good choice. We'll send you to the psychiatrist, then." Keeler wrote a name on a piece of paper and looked at Lane.

"Yes?" Lane asked.

"The indications are that Arthur's breast cancer is treatable. I've sent him to one of the best surgeons in North America. Even so, you're going to have to take care of yourself and be there for Arthur and the kids. If you have any questions, you call. Are we clear?"

Lane nodded.

"Mavis will call the psychiatrist and book an appointment for you." Keeler shook Lane's hand.

Ten minutes later, Lane sat in a coffee shop on Fourth Street. He watched the rush hour traffic — four-wheeled, two-wheeled, and two-legged — as it paraded past. His mind traveled back in time as he remembered Arthur's sister. How the cancer ate away at her until she was practically a skeleton, with Holocaust eyes.

"Mochaccino. Extra large. Extra hot!"

Lane got up, picked up his coffee, and sat back down. *I've got a couple of minutes*, he thought just as his phone rang. Lane set his coffee down and reached for the cell. "Hello?"

"Lane? It's Lori."

"You're at work early." *It's funny how cheerful I can sound when I'm supposed to be depressed.*

"Just got a call from the deputy chief's office."

Lane looked out the window as a police cruiser passed, with its flashing lights painting the inside of the coffee shop in shades of red and blue.

"The deputy chief wants to see you Monday morning at eight o'clock instead of this morning." Lori paused. "You got that?"

"I've got it. Thanks." Lane was about to hang up.

"Lane, wait! There's more."

"Okay — give it to me."

×

Lane pulled into a parking lot framed by a rectangle of shops. He parked in front of a business no more than three metres wide. The JELENA'S ALTERATIONS sign on the window was half a metre high and went the width of the glass. He closed the Chev's door and stretched. Through the open front door, he could see Jelena taking cash from a smiling young woman holding a wedding gown wrapped in clear plastic. Lane waited for the young woman to edge her way out the open door. She was careful not to allow the dress to drag on the ground or touch the doorframe.

He stepped inside.

"Detective!" Jelena crossed her arms.

Three women worked on sewing machines lining one wall at the back of the shop. Lane recognized a mixture of fear, anger, and curiosity on their faces as he stood across from Jelena, who leaned against the cash register. *She wants me to get the message that this is her turf,* Lane thought.

"You have more questions for me?" Jelena pushed the cash register closed.

Her implication is clear. She's showing the others I can't be trusted. "We've been doing some research on the name Borislav Goran."

Jelena glanced at the clock on the wall, then addressed the woman working at the first sewing machine. "Rasima! I'm for coffee." She grabbed a pack of cigarettes and led Lane out the door. "Coffee?"

Lane nodded then followed as she crossed the parking lot. She lit a cigarette. Lane kept to her right in order to avoid the cloud of exhaled smoke trailing behind her. "Where are we going?"

Jelena pointed her cigarette at a sub shop tucked between an ice cream shop and a furniture store. When they reached the sub shop, Lane opened the door, but Jelena sat down outside at a picnic table squatting on a tongue of grass jutting out into the pavement. "Tell Jordan that Jelena wants a coffee."

Lane stepped inside. Jordan was around twenty-five, blonde, with an athletic build.

"What would you like? I already know what Jelena wants—black coffee." Jordan smiled from behind a counter of meats, cheeses, and vegetables.

Lane looked at the coffee menu posted above the espresso machine. Jordan's specialty was a double shot of espresso, chocolate, caramel, and fresh cream. "I'll have the special," Lane said.

"Large?"

Lane nodded and looked over his shoulder at Jelena, who watched him through the window with her hunter's eyes while taking a drag from her cigarette.

"She's tough, but she's had no choice, in case you're wondering," Jordan said as he poured cream and chocolate milk into a metal cup with a thermometer hooked inside the lip.

Lane watched Jordan move with practiced efficiency as he measured coffee grounds for the espresso machine. "You know her well?"

"I opened my business at the same time she started over there. Gradually, we got to know one another. I send customers to her, and she does the same for me. She keeps her business going, takes care of herself and her daughter. Single mom making it work — you know the story."

"Sort of," Lane said.

"Her husband left about a year ago. He used to work the cash register in the shop when he was able." Jordan steamed the chocolate milk and cream.

"When he was able?"

"Alcoholic." Jordan poured the espresso into the milk and cream. Then he added a shot of caramel and put Lane's special on the counter. Jordan poured coffee from a carafe into a second cup. Lane handed over a twenty. Jordan made change. "Jelena came here after the war. She started over, raises a daughter, runs a business, and does it on her own. It hasn't been easy for her."

"Thanks." Lane took the change, tucked it into his pocket, and took the drinks outside.

Jelena stabbed her cigarette into an overfull ashtray and took her coffee. She closed her eyes when she tasted it. "Jordan makes good coffee."

Lane sipped his. *I have to agree.*

"What you want?" Jelena asked.

"Who's Borislav Goran?" Lane watched her eyes.

She looked through the window at Jordan. "Died in the war."

"He looks a lot like your husband," Lane said.

"Borislav was Andelko's cousin. We called him Bo. He liked that nickname." Jelena continued to look away.

"What did you and Andelko fight about before he left?"

She looked directly at Lane. "He drank too much. I got tired of it."

"Did he drink because of the war?"

Jelena reached for another cigarette. She lit it, inhaled, and blew her smoke away from the table. "Andelko saw a man downtown, at Eau Claire."

Lane waited. *Her answers sound rehearsed.*

"A juggler. It was on a weekend. Andelko saw the juggler, came home, got drunk, and we started to fight." She drank the last of her coffee.

"What was this juggler to Andelko?" Lane asked.

"Andelko said the juggler was going to kill him. He kept saying the juggler's name was Mladen."

×

"I need to find out all I can about Borislav Goran. Apparently he died in the war." Lane set a cup of lemon tea in front of Lori.

"So, give a girl a cup of tea and she'll do your work for you?" Lori smiled, ready for some verbal fencing.

"We both know you're the computer genius, and I'm hopeless at it. I need to know what's available on Borislav Goran and Andelko Branimir. Today I was told that Goran was a cousin of Branimir. If possible, that fact needs to be verified."

Lori leaned forward in her chair. She cocked her head to the left. Lane moved closer.

"Something's up. I don't know for sure what it is, but the deputy chief called Harper in. They met for most of the morning. Whatever it is, the whole building is buzzing with rumours." Lori leaned back in her chair.

Lane sat down in a wooden armchair. He sipped his cup of coffee. *Guess that means I'll be out of a job come Monday.* He shrugged. "I've got this case to solve."

"And you've got Arthur to worry about."

Lane tried to smile. "We see the surgeon in a week."

Gregory stepped into the office. He was wearing a white shirt and tie. His belly was a muffin top hanging over a black leather belt. He glared at Lane. "You getting paid to sit around?"

Stockwell followed Gregory into the office. He was wearing the high black boots and the jodhpurs of a motorcycle cop. He put his hands on his hips and looked down on Lane. "It's what the good detective does best — sits on his ass and drinks coffee." Stockwell's close-shaved head shone like Gregory's.

Gregory went into his office, followed by Stockwell, who closed the door.

Lori said, "Charming pair of assholes."

×

"Eau Claire? What time?" Christine asked.

They sat around the dinner table. Roz had her nose at Christine's elbow.

"Please stop feeding her from the table," Lane said.

Christine pointed her fork at Matt. "How was work at the golf course today?"

"Same old, same old. Bunkers and mowers." Matt speared a piece of chicken and sawed at it with his knife. His arms and face were a Mediterranean brown.

"At least you're getting a nice tan," Arthur said.

Lane spotted Christine as she took a piece of chicken from her plate and dropped her hand under the table. "Stop that!" Lane said.

"What?" Christine smiled innocently back at him. She blinked several times.

Lane shook his head.

Christine shrugged. "Roz likes chicken. When do you go to Eau Claire?"

"It's something I have to do for work."

"Isn't tomorrow your day off?" Arthur asked.

"Why don't we all go?" Christine asked.

"Good idea." Arthur cut a slice of chicken and added blueberries.

Good, blueberries are antioxidants, Lane thought.

"I've got the afternoon off," Matt said.

Anything to get away from here so we can think about something besides Arthur's cancer.

chapter 4

"You need to be at work this early?" Matt climbed to the top of the stairs. He wore his heavy khaki-coloured denim work pants and tan golf shirt.

Shit, Lane thought, *I forgot he gets up early to work for a few hours at the golf course.* "Couldn't sleep. Want a cup of coffee?" Lane slid his chair back.

"I'll get it." Matt reached into the fridge for chocolate milk. He poured it into a cup, and set it in the microwave.

"What are you doing?" Lane asked.

"I heat up the chocolate for forty-five seconds, then add coffee. Try it." Matt pulled the cup out of the microwave, filled the cup with coffee, and sipped.

"Want me to make you some breakfast?" Lane looked into his half-empty cup.

"It's Saturday. I buy breakfast at the snack shack on Saturdays." He sat down beside Lane at the table.

Lane looked out the window. *When kids get older, they get a life of their own.* The belly of an overcast sky was purple with a hint of pink. "Is Christine driving the beer cart today?"

"Tomorrow. There's some kind of tournament going on." Matt hesitated. "Uncle?"

Something in Matt's tone warned Lane he was about to say something important.

"What's going to happen to Uncle Arthur?" Matt looked out the window.

"All I can tell you is I think it will be okay. Everybody says I'm depressed, but I think it will all work out fine," Lane said.

×

Matt must think I'm crazy, Lane thought as he sat in the driver's seat at a red light. He looked to his left.

The female passenger in the adjacent pickup truck looked down and smiled. Her hair was blonde, her full lips were red, and she was smoking a cigar.

Lane smiled back. *I'm talking to myself. The doctor is right, I do need a shrink. That's on the to-do list, right after Arthur beating cancer and finding out who killed Andelko Branimir.*

The light turned green. The pickup roared ahead, leaving behind a cloud of diesel smoke. Lane changed lanes before turning left. Towering condos and hotels gathered along the south side of the Bow River around an upscale enclave called Eau Claire. It was the area of the water park, the bridge to Princess Island, and the concourse in between that Lane was headed for.

He parked the car in front of a hotel across the street from a restaurant that had, at one time, been home to a lumber mill. It was ten in the morning and the sun was forcing its way through the clouds, promising a rare warm, summery day. *Glad I didn't wear a sports jacket,* Lane thought as his phone rang. He pulled it out of his pocket. "Hello."

"Where are you?" Christine asked.

"Eau Claire, looking for street performers." Lane looked around at the people on bicycles and rollerblades weaving around the walkers and joggers and wheelchairs.

"We're coming too." Christine hung up.

At the wading pool, kids aimed water guns at one another. Adults dressed in shorts or rolled-up pants were bent over, holding the arms of toddlers who splashed the water with their feet.

A trumpet blasted a saucy salsa tune. Lane looked toward the source of the sound. The trumpet player leaned on one crutch. He wore a red T-shirt, shoes, and shorts. His red cap was turned backwards.

"It's Leo," Lane said under his breath.

The Latino music turned heads. A pair of toddlers began to dance. Lane smiled at their natural grace and total lack of self-consciousness.

Lane spotted a juggler. He was taller than Leo, but close to the same weight. He was black-haired, and wore a white loose-fitting shirt and knee-length shorts. He began to juggle four knives. The sun flashed on the metal blades as each knife spun to the top of its arc before falling back into the man's hand, only to be launched again into the sky. The knives and the juggler moved to the trumpeter's beat.

Soon the music stopped. The knives fell. The juggler caught them neatly and stashed them in his equipment bag. He looked around at the crowd. "I need a young assistant."

Parents looked at one another. Children waited for the music to start up again so they could dance. A teenaged brother pushed his little sister — she was about five and wore a blue jumper and running shoes — out into the open. Lane noted the butterfly painted on her face.

The juggler bent down to her. She whispered something to him. "This is Katie, my new assistant!" He walked her to the edge of the crowd. "Show your appreciation for Katie!"

Katie's brother stood and encouraged the crowd to clap and cheer. Leo played a tune that sounded like it belonged at a bullfight. Katie smiled and walked a little taller.

The juggler bent over his bag and pulled out a sword. "Katie?"

She looked up at him. Leo played louder, faster. Now it was the music of a warrior.

"Would you hold this for me?" The juggler handed her the sword. "Here, with two hands." He showed her how to hold the sword so that it was at a right angle to the ground. Then he turned, reached into his bag, and pulled out a basketball. He spun it on his finger as he walked around Katie. He spun the ball one last time and placed it on the tip of the sword before bowing to Katie and backing away.

She stood there for a full thirty seconds with the ball spinning and the crowd cheering. The ball fell off. The juggler caught it after the first bounce. "Everyone! I give you Katie!"

Leo blasted notes of triumph from his trumpet. Katie handed the sword to the juggler and walked to join her brother, who put a proud arm around her shoulder.

The juggler put the basketball into his bag and pulled out a blue glass ball the size and irregular shape of a cantaloupe. He held the glass in the air, allowing the audience to appreciate its fragile beauty. He reached for a unicycle made ready by Leo. Once balanced on the bike, the juggler walked the lopsided ball from the palm of his right hand to the back of the hand, up his forearm, across his shoulders, and down his left arm as Leo's trumpet sang a saucy number.

A flash of sunlight on metal caught Lane's eye. He stared at the juggler's right leg. Just below the man's knee was a flesh-coloured cup connected to a shaft of metal reaching a plastic foot. *He's doing all of this on one good leg!*

The audience clapped as the juggler pretended to lose his balance. He fell off the bike, flipped the glass melon in the air, recovered, and caught the lopsided globe mere millimetres from the concrete. He stood, raised the globe over his head, smiled, and threw it to the ground. It bounced into the hands of a surprised woman in the front row.

Applause and laughter erupted.

Leo took off his cap to lay it on the ground at the juggler's feet. Bills and coins dropped into the cap. Lane waited for the crowd around the hat to thin before he dropped in his contribution. He studied the juggler more closely. The man looked to be about twenty-five. He drank from a bottle of water and wiped his face with a towel. The juggler sensed Lane's interest and returned the detective's stare.

"Detective? That you?" Leo leaned on his crutch with his right hand as he swept up the cap with his left. The trumpet hung from a strap around his neck in much the same way his withered right leg hung a few centimetres above the pavement.

"How are you, Leo?"

"Mladen and I are doing really well as long as the sun keeps shining." Leo handed the cap to the juggler, who emptied the money into a cloth bag, which he pulled closed with a string before dropping it into his equipment bag.

Lane kept his attention on Mladen. "Do you have time to talk between shows?"

Leo looked at Mladen. "What's it about?"

Mladen shrugged. "I was going to grab a coffee." He looked over to the terrace near the coffee shop, where tables sat under faded green umbrellas.

His accent sounds like Spanish mixed with something else. "Works for me."

"Okay." Leo didn't sound convinced. "What's this about?"

"A murder." Lane waited for the pair to gather their equipment. *We must look odd—me pushing a unicycle, Leo with his crutch and trumpet, and Mladen with his bag of tricks and artificial leg. Somehow, though, it feels about right.*

Lane leaned the unicycle up against the red brick wall next to an empty table. He waited and watched over the equipment until the two performers returned with their coffees. Then Lane went off to buy his own. *All of this done without a single word.*

Mladen sat with his back to the brick wall. He sipped his espresso while studying the crowd.

Leo had his crutch propped up against the table and was watching Lane as if challenging the detective to speak first. Lane attempted to look where Mladen was staring. The detective squinted at the glare of the sun upon the water in the wading pool.

"What murder?" Mladen asked.

"A body was found in the northwest in a slough at the edge of the city. The man's name was Andelko Branimir." Lane turned to study Mladen's face.

Mladen met the detective's gaze. "Don't know him."

Try a different approach. "How do you and Leo know each other?"

"We met at the doctor's office," Leo said. "We go to the same specialist. We got talking about street performing and decided to make some extra money on weekends."

Lane turned to Mladen. "Where did you learn to be a juggler?"

"Malabarista." Mladen studied Lane's reaction.

"Malabarista?"

"He was trained in Spain at a school for jugglers. Over there he was called a malabarista." Leo looked at Mladen to see if he'd said too much. Mladen allowed no visible reaction.

"Before or after the accident?" Lane pointed at Mladen's artificial leg.

"No accident," Mladen said.

"He lost it in a war." Leo shifted in his chair. "How come you're asking us about this Andelko guy?"

"I was told that Andelko was afraid of a juggler who works at Eau Claire, so I came to take a look around." Lane watched Mladen.

"Malabarista." Mladen smiled.

"So," Leo said, "who sent you after two dangerous one-legged street performers?"

Quick, before this becomes one big joke! "The victim may have gone by another name: Borislav Goran."

Mladen's face went white. His shoulders and head sagged. "Pinche bastard!"

Lane, stunned by the reaction, leaned back in his chair.

"Pinche pendejo!" Mladen said.

"Who was Goran?" Lane asked.

"Murderer! Rapist! Laughing! Laughing! All the time laughing! Él mató a mi padre! Drunken pig!" Mladen stood, lifted the table with its umbrella, and threw it over Lane and Leo's heads, showering them with what remained of the coffee, then picked up his bag and unicycle and stomped away.

Leo looked at Lane after they got untangled from the table, chairs, and umbrella. "Man, you sure know how to screw up a beautiful day."

Lane picked up his spilled coffee cup. "Last name?"

"What?" Leo picked up his crutch.

"Mladen's last name?" Lane tossed the cup into a nearby garbage can.

Leo shook his head. "Why?"

"Because this isn't over."

"Do you have any idea what you've just done?" Leo tucked the crutch under his arm.

Lane waited.

"Asshole." Leo turned his back and walked away.

"You okay?" Matt asked.

Lane turned.

"We came to take a look around," Christine said.

"And keep an eye on you," Arthur said with a smile.

"We should have brought you a change of clothes," Matt said.

"Join us for a cup of coffee?" Arthur asked.

Matt and Christine righted the table.

Unaccountably, Lane found himself on the verge of tears.

×

"You never said why those street performers acted the way they did." Christine stood next to the closet across from the front door.

Lane caught the scent of strawberries and noticed Christine's hair braided at the back of her neck and her low-cut white T-shirt and lipstick. "Where are you off to?"

She eased past him. "I'm gonna meet some friends from school. A couple of them have the same class with me in the fall. Now answer *my* question."

"I asked him something that made him angry," Lane said.

"Whatever." Christine shook her head and shut the door behind her.

Lane kicked his shoes off and stepped into the kitchen. Arthur was in the backyard with Roz. Both were digging in separate flowerbeds.

Lane went upstairs to change clothes, then downstairs to throw his coffee-stained shirt, pants, and socks in the wash. Matt's room was across from the laundry room. He could hear snoring through the closed door.

The phone rang after Lane turned on the washing machine. He ran upstairs, searched the kitchen for his cell phone, and found it where he'd left it, under the newspaper. "Hello."

"Colin Weaver here. I have some updates on the remains of Andelko Branimir."

Lane thought he heard some emotion breaking through Fibre's usual monotone. *You've become a man of surprises*, Lane thought. "Go ahead."

"A fractured skull and the resultant blunt force trauma to the brain is the most likely cause of death. After we measured the remains, we found that the height matched that of Branimir. And we will try a computer-generated image of the victim's face to see if it matches the picture on the driver's license. So far, that's what we have." Fibre waited.

"You're being very thorough with this one," Lane said.

"I like to be exact." Fibre hung up.

Lane leaned his head back on the couch and listened to the hum of the washing machine and Matt's snoring.

Lane closed his eyes. *I feel like a nap.*

"Uncle?" Matt asked.

Lane opened his eyes. Matt was leaning over him and shaking his shoulder.

"After I get home from work tomorrow, can we take the dog for a walk down by the river?"

"What time is it?" Lane asked.

"After seven. Uncle Arthur saved some supper for you." Matt turned and went upstairs. Lane followed. He found Arthur asleep in the living room armchair.

Dinner was on a plate wrapped in tinfoil in the oven. The chicken, rice, and corn were still edible, but Lane found he'd lost his ability to taste or enjoy food.

After supper, he scraped most of the food into the garbage and put the dishes into the dishwasher. *Might just as well go to bed,* he thought. Just then, he heard a key in the lock of the back door. The hinges creaked as the door opened. Christine stepped inside. There was a red mark under her left eye. The eye was well on its way to becoming swollen shut.

"What happened to you?" Lane moved closer to her.

"Nothin'." She looked at the floor. She was favouring her right arm.

"I'll get some ice."

"I just want to go to my room." Christine tried to push past him.

"After we get some ice on the eye and I take a look at your arm." He hugged her close when she began to cry.

×

"I told you I don't want to be here! I'm fine!" Christine turned to Lane. They sat side by side at the Foothills Medical Centre Emergency waiting room.

"We'll get you checked out, just to be on the safe side. And after it's documented, I'll find out who did this, and I'll hunt him down."

"Look, he was drunk. I told him I didn't want to ride home with him. He grabbed me by the arm, I told him to let go, then he hit me in the face." Christine took the bag of ice away from her face and gingerly touched the skin around her eye. "I keep telling you it's taken care of."

A woman's voice reached out to the entire room full of waiting people. "I still don't understand how you could go out for a cup of coffee with friends and end up getting drunk and being assaulted!"

Lane and Christine turned to witness the drama, just like everyone else.

The mother was just over five feet and weighed maybe one hundred and forty pounds. The son was over six feet. His brown hair was frosted, and he wore a tight mauve T-shirt. The front of his shirt was stained with blood. He was using crutches. There were stitches in his lower lip, which was swollen to at least three times its normal size. "I told you," he said. "I fell down, hit my face on a curb, and then Rob drove me to the hospital."

Christine developed a sudden interest in looking at her toes and holding the bag of ice against her nose.

"Don't lie to me! I can tell when you're lying to me!" the mother said.

The son looked around the waiting room as if checking to see if he knew anyone. His eyes focused on Christine. He halted.

Lane felt emotion toss good judgment aside. He stood. Christine grabbed his arm. The mother and son went out the sliding glass doors. Lane broke Christine's grip. He followed the mother and son outside.

"What's your name?" Lane waited for the pair to turn around.

"What's it to you?" the son asked.

"Christine is my niece. You assaulted her!" Lane stepped closer.

The son looked over Lane's shoulder and spotted Christine. "She did this to me!" He looked pleadingly at his mother.

"Leave it alone, uncle." Christine grabbed the back of Lane's shirt.

The mother looked confused. "You said you fell."

"He called me a bitch, then punched me." Christine pointed at her eye. "I hit him in the mouth and took out his knee."

The woman looked at her son. She turned to lead him toward the parking lot.

"She hit me," he repeated.

Lane followed them. Christine grabbed him by the back of his shirt. When her feet began to slide on the cement, she grabbed a No Parking sign and held on. "Uncle!"

The mother seemed to shrink as she turned. She looked at her son and dropped her eyes. "Please, leave us alone," she said to Lane. "Let me take care of this."

Lane and Christine walked across the overfull parking lot. After at least five minutes of silence, Lane put the key in the ignition. "You did that?"

"He showed up drunk. When I told him I didn't want a ride home, he got mean. He grabbed my arm. I pushed him away. He took a swing at me and hit me in the eye. Then I hit him in the mouth and took out his knee, just the way you taught me."

She sounds as tired and defeated as I feel.

They drove home in the darkness of the summer evening. Moonlight reflected off oil stains on the pavement, making them shimmer like black puddles of water.

"When do you think it'll rain?" Christine asked.

Lane shrugged.

"It hurts when you shut us out like this. You know that Uncle Arthur cries in the morning after you leave? I hear him when I wake up. He pretends like he's not upset, but I can tell. It hurts him. It hurts us all. As if we don't have enough to worry about with Uncle Arthur's cancer. That's why I didn't want to make a big deal about this." Christine's eyes filled with tears.

Lane started to say something but thought better of it.

"Uncle's worried about you, and so am I." Christine opened her window and stuck the ice bag outside. The hot air buffeted the inside of the Jeep as she opened the knot in the bag to let the water leak away.

Lane looked in the rear-view mirror. There was a splash of silver on the pavement. His eyes were reflected in the mirror. He saw and felt them filling with tears.

chapter 5

"Uncle Arthur and Christine went shopping. We're going down by the river. There's something you have to see." Matt was scooping up the supper dishes. They clattered against each other as he stuffed them in the dishwasher, deep lines creasing his forehead. There was an intensity to every move Matt made.

"You're the boss." Lane handed Matt the salad bowl.

Matt stopped and looked over his shoulder. "And this boss says we talk about your depression and Uncle Arthur's cancer."

I opened the door, Lane thought. "Fair enough."

Roz rode in the back and whined whenever they passed anything resembling a park. She scooted from one side of the Jeep to the other, sticking her nose against the glass.

"So, you gonna start talking or am I?" Matt drove with the seat pushed almost as far forward as it would go. He wore his glasses and refused to take his eyes off the road.

"Okay. What do you know about the fight Christine got into?" Lane watched for any change in Matt's expression and was rewarded with a frown.

"The guy was drunk, he came on to her, and she took care of it." Matt smiled.

"That's all that she told you?"

Matt let out a long sigh. "Not all. Some she asked me to keep private."

"Do I need to be worried about what I don't know?"

"If I say no, will you stop worrying?" Matt glanced at his uncle.

"Probably not."

"What she told me to keep private is nothing you need to worry about — at least not yet." Matt smiled.

"Thanks a lot," Lane said.

"Well, you did say that Christine and I need to trust each other. Do you want me to break that trust?" Matt turned off the pavement and onto the gravel road bisecting the park. He grimaced when he failed to avoid a pothole.

"No. How come you remember everything I say?" Lane held onto the door handle as the Jeep bucked.

Matt shrugged. "I don't know. I just do."

"I don't think that what happened to your Mom is going to happen to Arthur." Lane remembered the weight she'd lost in the final weeks of her cancer. *That can't happen to Arthur!*

Roz whined when she realized where they were.

"I hope not." Matt pulled into a parking space. The dust from the gravel road gathered around the Jeep. He shut off the engine and got out.

They opened the back hatch to let Roz out. She wheezed at the end of the leash. "Come on," Matt said as the dog dragged him along behind her.

Lane followed them to a paved path that headed toward the river before turning east to parallel the water. Lane felt the cooler air carried by a breeze from the west. He looked to the bluff where Douglas firs climbed up one hundred metres to the homes in the neighbourhood of Wildwood.

Matt shifted his grip. Roz coughed and pulled.

"Where are we going?" Lane asked.

"It's not very far." Matt threw the comment over his shoulder as Roz lunged forward.

They could hear geese honking ahead and to their left. Lane watched a pair of Canada geese join the flock of birds already gathered on the green expanse between the soccer field and river pathway. "I used to do this at home," Matt said, "when the geese gathered in the early fall. It made me feel like I could do anything, you know. If I was feeling down, if my dad made me feel like I didn't exist, I'd just go into the field and wait until they landed." His voice was high-pitched with anticipation. He held on tight to Roz's leash.

"You used to do what?" Lane looked at the geese and then the river. *Are we going to jump off the bank?*

"Ready?" Matt stared at Lane.

"For what?"

Roz lunged, pulling Matt along behind. The dog ran with fluid power, her ears pointed forward and her tail a straight line. Matt ran with one leg catching up to the other, his trailing foot aimed off at odd angles. It looked as if, at any moment, he might trip and fall face-forward onto the grass.

Lane began to run. He was a little to the right of Roz and Matt.

The geese began to honk. Soon, Lane and Matt were side by side. Matt dropped the leash and Roz dodged left, forcing the flock in front of Matt and Lane.

There must be over one hundred birds.

Their wings began to flap as they waddled, then ran. Lane was almost among the birds. He looked at Matt. Pure joy deepened the lines around his nephew's eyes. Matt let out a cry of exhilaration as the geese began to lift off.

Lane could feel the air pushed by their wings. He looked right. A goose was flying beside him, honking. The tip of its wing brushed Lane's shoulder. Geese surrounded him now. Their necks bobbed as they worked to gain altitude. Lane felt as if he were about lift off as well. The wind kissed his face. The flock was all around him. For a moment, he was part of the undulating mass of Canadian geese. Lane screamed with unexpected joy.

A minute later, Roz came back, her tongue hanging out one side of her mouth. Matt was bent over, his hands on his knees, trying to catch his breath.

Lane inhaled and watched the flock as it turned west, then south over the river. "Amazing!" he said.

Matt smiled at his uncle. "Makes you feel alive, doesn't it? Like you could fly!" He threw his arms up and laughed.

"I think I'm going to get fired tomorrow." The words were out before Lane could reel them back in.

Matt stared. "You sure?"

"I made the chief look bad when we arrested one of his buddies. You remember the dentist who was into little girls?"

Matt nodded.

"He was one of Chief Smoke's buddies. That's why Smoke put me under investigation. It's not about the weapon at all."

"It's all about Smoke's ego?"

"Pretty much."

"When you think about it, you are being punished for doing your job." There was a note of incredulity in Matt's voice.

Lane shrugged.

"What else?" Matt asked.

Lane shook his head. "My brother and his wife offered money for Christine's education, but I said no."

"Why?"

Lane watched the flock circle back. "Because they wouldn't do the same for you."

"Why not just take the money for Christine?"

"They acted like you didn't count. Like you and Christine and Arthur aren't my real family."

"Oh." Matt waited a moment then asked, "Are you sure Uncle Arthur will be okay?"

chapter 6

Police Chief Under the Influence

Calgary Chief of Police Calvin Smoke was charged with driving under the influence in the early hours of yesterday morning. Smoke was attending an international conference for police chiefs in San Diego, California when he was charged.

A spokesperson for the San Diego Police Department reported that Smoke registered 2.1, more than twice the legal limit for alcohol concentration in the blood stream.

Recently, Chief Smoke's reputation has been tarnished by his association with Doctor Joseph Jones, who was charged with the murder of his dental assistant. Jones was also implicated in a child pornography ring.

"Matt told me you're upset because you think you're going to get fired." Arthur sat in a kitchen chair. His coffee cup sat in front of him. The cup was almost big enough for Roz to use as a drinking dish.

"You've been so busy. Taking on extra clients so we can pay for the kids' education. I didn't think you needed more on your plate. And now you've got breast cancer. My worries pale by comparison." *Now that I've said it, it sounds so lame*, Lane thought.

"Give me a break! Do you have any idea what it's been like around here?" Arthur's voice rose with anger until it seemed like it could shatter ceramic.

"I live here." Lane thought the offhand remark might defuse the situation.

"Oh, really? That's what you call what you've been doing?" Arthur's sarcasm was accentuated by his body language.

"You are such a drama queen!" *Okay, let's go for it!*

"Finally!" Arthur threw his arms in the air.

"What are you talking about now?" Lane found himself floundering.

"You're talking to me. Saying what's on your mind. Do you realize how long it's been since we had any kind of real conversation? Do you think I can beat this fucking disease on my own?" Arthur looked sideways at Lane.

Answer this the right way or you'll be in more trouble. Go with the first question. "A week?"

"Ten days."

"I'm sorry." Lane looked at the stove clock. *I'd better get moving.*

"And after you get fired, if you do in fact get fired, I expect to meet you for lunch."

"A celebration?" Lane was surprised, not for the fist time that day.

"Why not? I won't miss what this job does to your head, and what it does to us. Besides, who knows how long either one of us has?"

×

Lane replayed their conversation in his mind as he parked downtown behind the barbed wire of the police compound alongside the offices of Calgary Police Services.

Five minutes later, he stepped off the elevator and onto the floor where Deputy Chief Simpson's office was located. An officer pushing a dolly piled high with boxes brushed past Lane to get into the elevator.

Lane found the deputy chief's office. More boxes and a computer sat in stacks on various chairs in the waiting room. A young woman wearing blue jeans and a T-shirt sat next to the computer. She pushed a wayward strand of red hair back over her ears and studied Lane with frank fascination.

She's watching the detective get fired. Word sure gets around in this place, he thought.

Lane could see the feet of another woman on her knees under the receptionist's desk. He coughed.

The woman backed out and looked up at Lane. Her hair was grey and short. She looked to be about fifty. "Yes?"

It's a good thing you're wearing pants, girl. "Detective Lane to see —"

"Go right in, he's waiting for you," she said before turning her attention back to whatever she was looking for under the desk.

Lane walked to the open door. He looked inside. Deputy Chief Simpson was sitting at his desk, working the keys on his laptop. Lane looked around. The walls were free of pictures and the shelves were empty. The carpet was pitted with the imprints of missing furniture.

Simpson looked up. His blond hair was cut short. His blue

eyes studied Lane with obvious curiosity. He stood, leaned over the desk, and offered his hand.

Lane shook it. The officers took the measure of one another.

"Please close the door." Simpson's voice was friendly and commanding. "We have to get this done today."

Lane shut the door and turned to face Simpson, who stepped around to the front of the desk.

"We have a problem," Simpson said, "and Deputy Chief Harper thinks you're the solution."

Deputy Chief Harper? What is he talking about? "What?"

"Did you read this morning's newspaper?"

"No." *What am I missing here? I thought he called me in to fire me.*

"Chief Smoke resigned early this morning. I've been asked to act as chief. And I've asked for Cam Harper to take on the duties of deputy chief. He accepted." Simpson waited for Lane to process the news.

"This is not what I expected." Lane frowned when his voice broke.

"What were you expecting?" Simpson's phone rang. He ignored it.

"Because I'm being investigated, I assumed I was being terminated."

Simpson thought for a moment, as if considering what to say next. "Since word circulated of the investigation into your conduct, four distinguished officers, an elder from the Tsuu T'ina Nation, two doctors, and a local lawyer have been very insistent about making appointments with me to vouch for you, your character, and your contributions to this community. Frankly, terminating you is the furthest thing from my mind."

Lane considered what Simpson had said and his calm delivery of the message.

"You understand that once the investigation into this so-called lost weapon was initiated, the process had to be followed through to its conclusion?"

Lane nodded.

"That's about as much as I can say at this time without running the risk of jeopardizing the process." Simpson leaned his right hand on his desk.

"Well then?" Lane moved to leave, but Simpson stopped him.

"We haven't talked about the problem," he said with a smile.

"Problem?"

"I have a young officer on loan from the RCMP. She's right outside. She worked undercover for several months at a local restaurant. Her instincts are good, she's bright, and the new deputy chief assures me that she will be an excellent detective — with the right kind of training, of course. Frankly, we'd like to get her on here permanently. As of yet, you haven't been assigned a new partner." Simpson smiled again. "You understand, of course, that this is not an order?"

"Right now, there's very little that I do understand." Lane wished he had a cup of coffee.

"She's made some powerful people unhappy because of the evidence she uncovered. Sound familiar?" Simpson waited for Lane to catch up. "We need an experienced detective to work with her and protect her."

"Protect her?"

"Threats have been made against her life."

×

Arthur sat on the terrace behind the coffee shop in Kensington. It overlooked an alley and a residential street where new houses were replacing old ones and trees reached across the road to touch one another. He studied Lane through his sunglasses as he arrived on the terrace accompanied by a young woman. Lane grabbed an extra chair and sat next to him.

"Arthur, meet Keely Saliba." Lane indicated with his open right hand that it was safe to talk openly with her.

Arthur leaned across the table to shake hands. "And?"

Keely turned her blue eyes on Lane. "We're partners," he said.

Arthur took a sip from his coffee cup and set it down again. "So you weren't fired?"

Keely shook her head. "Smoke was."

"Chief Smoke?" Arthur looked at Lane and then at Keely.

"Resigned due to an impaired driving charge in San Diego." Keely looked over her shoulder as their coffees arrived.

"Keely Saliba?" Arthur blinked. He was having difficulty catching up with the turn of events.

"That's right. My mom's of Irish descent. My dad's from Lebanon." Keely waited to see if Arthur was up to speed yet. "Mom's a lawyer. Dad's a teacher. I have a brother. I was in the RCMP for a year when I was asked to work undercover in a restaurant. When that job was done, Harper and Simpson came up with the idea that I should be Detective Lane's new partner."

"Cam Harper?" Arthur asked.

"Big guy? Big mustache?" Keely asked.

"That's him." Lane wanted to laugh but felt sorry for Arthur, who was bouncing from one surprise to the next.

"The restaurant where I was undercover was upscale. Lots of the city's who's who would show up there. Simpson wanted me to pay special attention to the Scotch drinkers' club. There were leaks in the department, and he wanted to find out if the restaurant was the source. It turned out the leaks were coming from Smoke's ever-expanding drinkers' club." Keely put her hand over her mouth and pulled it away. "Arthur, you're not a cop. I shouldn't be telling you this!"

"No, but he might as well be," Lane said.

"How do you like the coffee?" Arthur lifted his cup. "One of the perks of Lane's job. He finds all the best places for an excellent cup of coffee. It's where he gets much of his information. Kind of like you being a waitress at the Scotch drinkers' club. People talk as if there's no one else in the room. All you have to do is sit down, enjoy the coffee, and listen."

Keely looked at Lane. "Arthur's getting up to speed."

Lane nodded. He looked past Keely as a young woman in a red tank top approached with plates of food.

They devoured their soup, salad, and sandwiches in silence. Patrons began to occupy nearby tables. Lane looked over the alley at the trees and then the shrubs below. He wondered about past cases and thought, *What will I remember when I look back on this one?*

"When will you tell me about the case you're working on?" Keely asked, wiping her lips with a napkin.

"Our case." Lane watched the breeze play with the leaves on the trees in front of the newly constructed mansions eyeing each other from across the street. He turned to see that another strand of Keely's red hair had freed itself and was now hanging in front of her eyes. She blew it away. It fell back down. *She's only a bit older than Christine.*

"I don't understand." Keely again wiped her mouth with a napkin. Her blue eyes zeroed in on him.

"If we're partners, then it's 'our' case."

Keely smiled, then hid her reaction behind a hand.

Arthur leaned back in his chair to give Lane and Keely their space. He acted like an outsider on the inside.

"Well then, tell me about *our* case," she said.

Lane leaned in close and kept his voice low. "The body of a male, we believe it to be Andelko Branimir, was found chained to cinder blocks in a dried-up slough. His wife says he bought a ticket to fly home last year. She says he had a drinking problem. Jelena, the wife, and her daughter live on the western edge of town."

"How far from where the body was found?" Keely asked.

Lane studied her. *Good question.* "Less than ten kilometres."

Keely nodded.

"Jelena says she and Andelko fought—"

"What kind of fight?" Keely asked.

Lane bristled at the interruptions. "—and he said he was going back home. She said he was upset after seeing someone from the war. A malabarista."

"Malabarista?"

"Juggler. Street performer. I found him at Eau Claire on Saturday morning. Everything was fine until I mentioned Goran's name."

"Goran?"

You don't miss much. "Two IDs were found with the remains: Branimir and Goran."

Keely nodded thoughtfully and leaned back in her chair.

"Exactly who has been threatening you?" Lane watched Keely's eyes as she mentally shifted gears from one case to another.

She looked north into the distance. "Don't know for certain. There have been anonymous threatening letters. Could be the guy who owned the restaurant where I worked undercover."

"Where is he?" Lane asked.

She shook her head. "Don't know. He's part of a biker gang that used the restaurant to launder money from the drug trade. He had some pictures of his biker buddies up in his office."

Lane sensed her hesitation. "What kinds of pictures?"

"Guys sitting on Harleys adorned with big-breasted women showing lots of cleavage. A couple of his associates turned out to be big boys in the biker hierarchy. The Scotch drinkers' club gave them advance warning of police investigations."

"Smoke was an even bigger idiot than I thought," Lane said.

Keely nodded. "Apparently, Smoke still is." She turned her head to one side. "Did you get the name of the juggler?"

"First names only. Leo plays music while Mladen does the juggling. Two men and two legs." Lane lifted his shoulders with a shrug.

"What do you mean?" Keely leaned forward.

"One has an artificial leg. The other has a withered leg."

Keely smiled. "We should be able to track down their last names easily enough."

I think I can see what Simpson and Harper were thinking. This one's got a quick mind for this kind of work.

×

The family sat on their backyard deck in the shade of the neighbour's house. "How come you picked such a loser?" Matt blanched when he heard the blunt tone of his question to Christine. Matt was so tanned that the creases around his eyes looked white in the valleys.

Lane and Arthur readied themselves for an explosion from Christine. They glanced at one another across a table covered with a tablecloth and a variety of salads.

Christine chewed her food deliberately, considering the question. "I don't know." She challenged Matt with her glare. Her eye was puffy, a purple bruise tattooed on her eyelid and cheek.

"I mean," Matt began slowly, "I always thought I had to prove myself to my dad, be a man. Be who he wanted me to be. You know how badly parents screw their kids up with messed-up expectations? Now I think maybe he had something to prove to me."

Christine winced. "I thought the guy was nice, but he turned out to be a jerk."

"It's just that women seem to go for the bad boy, you know? Look at my mom — she went for a jerk. I mean what's that all about?"

"I wish I knew." Christine looked at Roz, panting in the shade.

"What's exciting about getting beat up, or having to burn down a house and run away from a place where you're being treated like shit?" Matt looked in Roz's direction.

Christine's voice trembled. "I don't know, okay?"

"We've all got stuff to figure out." Lane said, reaching for a sweating glass of beer.

"Speaking of which, you've got an appointment with a psychiatrist." Arthur pointed his fork at Lane. "Tuesday morning."

"And what are we going to say to the surgeon on Friday?" Lane asked.

"You're coming with me?"

"Of course."

chapter 7

Lane looked across the low, round table at Dr. Alexandre. She looked, smelled, and sounded like a blonde southern belle. Her white blouse was ruffled and buttoned at the throat. She wore blue slacks and pumps. There were wedding and engagement rings on the appropriate finger of her left hand. She kept her hands in her lap. The scent of lavender permeated the air of her office.

"Thanks for the coffee." He raised his cup and smiled.

"Loraine said you're a very humane man underneath it all. That you've somehow managed to hold onto that despite what you've experienced." Dr. Alexandre's smile was gone.

Lane put the cup down. *So even my friends are involved. It begins.*

"She said that your family excommunicated you." Dr. Alexandre put air quotes around "excommunicated." "She also said you probably wouldn't want to talk with me."

To hell with it! If she wants the story, she gets it all. "Just after I came out to my family, none of my calls to them were being returned. I left messages, but. . . I drove over to my parents' house. It was around eight on a Sunday morning. I had a gift with me. It was Father's Day. The lights were on in the kitchen and my brother's car was parked out front. I knocked on the back door. There were footsteps on the stairs. I could see a silhouette through the translucent glass of the door. When I went to open the door, it was locked. I tried my key, but the lock had been changed. I knocked and tried the door again. There was the voice of my sister-in-law on the other side of the door, but I couldn't make out what she was saying. So I hung the gift on the doorknob and left. Haven't been back since."

"What did it feel like?"

Lane shrugged. "It turned out to be a blessing. I was on my own, and there was no turning back." *I wonder if she'll buy that.*

"How did it feel to be locked out of the house you grew up in?"

Lane shook his head, unable to get the words out.

"I have another appointment soon. Can we meet again tomorrow morning? Same time?" Dr. Alexandre leaned forward. The collar of her blouse opened enough for Lane to see a prominent Adam's apple.

"Okay." Lane answered without considering what he'd just discovered. "Are you going to peel me like an onion?"

Dr. Alexandre studied Lane before responding. "Some people call it peeling an onion. I don't. It's more like juggling — the past, the present, and what we fear or hope will happen in the future. Then more stuff gets added. Eventually we need to learn how to start again when all of the balls hit the floor. And with you, it appears there is a massive amount of juggling going on."

×

"You haven't said much." Keely sat at Harper's old desk next to Lane. She wore a black jacket, slacks, and white blouse. Her hair was tied back. "We haven't found out much besides the fact that a guy named Borislav Goran was accused of war crimes. So far, we've found ourselves short of specifics and big on generalizations."

Lane thought, *That's not what she meant, but. . .*

"That's not what I meant. I meant you seem distracted. You have a lot on your mind." She tapped her mouse and studied the computer screen.

"So you think you can read me?"

"Well, yes, since you asked." Keely kept her eyes on the screen.

"Yes, there's a lot on my mind."

"I checked you out, you know. Some of the people I talked with said I lucked out to be able to work with you and a few said. . ." She glanced his way, and her face reddened as she realized she'd said too much.

"Finish the sentence." Lane felt his deeply hidden emotions bracing for an impact.

"They say that you've never been promoted after making detective. That you play by your own rules, and that could be bad for my career, such as it is."

"That's all?" Lane watched Keely glance away.

Keely smiled and shook her head. "You're playing with me."

"Only a little. Look, you see if you can find out the malabarista Mladen's last name, and I'll walk down the hall to get some help with finding out more about Goran." He stood up and walked to the door. "I'll see if another resource is available." He stepped out the door.

Lane found Lori at her desk. She looked up at him from behind pink-framed glasses.

"How was the anniversary dinner?" Lane asked.

"The kids cooked for us. It was nice. They even did the dishes." She leaned left and looked past him. "How's the new partner working out?"

"Hard to tell at this point. Some of her friends tell her I'm going to be bad for her career." Lane smiled.

Lori laughed. "She might be right you know, except for. . ."

"Yes?" Lane waited for the joke he knew was coming.

"Your last partner ended up becoming deputy chief!"

Lane tilted his head one way, looked thoughtful, then rubbed his chin. "How come I didn't think of that?"

"You detectives always miss the obvious." Lori chuckled. "Isn't that what Matt and Christine always say?"

"I need to get some information on war crimes."

"The Hague?" Lori was all business now.

"Do you know any sites?" Lane sat on the edge of her desk.

"I'll ask around. You two go get a coffee, bring me back a mochaccino, and we'll see what I can find out." Lori reached into the bottom drawer of her desk and pulled out an aluminum ice cube tray. Lori turned red as she looked up at Lane. "It came out of my mother's fridge, okay? It's where I keep business cards. Now go and get my coffee!"

Ten minutes later, Lane and Keely walked side by side up the open-air mall running east and west through the heart of downtown.

"Sniffing out another coffee shop?" Keely lifted her nose as they walked west.

"It's just up here." He stopped at a red light and waited. A man pushing a shopping cart looked their way, then leaned over, picked a bottle out of a garbage can, and tucked it into a white plastic bag inside the cart.

Keely looked at the sign outside of a restaurant across the street. "The Diner? Now that's original."

"Good breakfast and great coffee." Lane anticipated the light changing, crossed the street, and held the door of The Diner open for her. He glanced over his shoulder as he heard the shopping cart's wheels rumbling over the bricks of the mall.

Inside, Jen was behind the cash register. She gave Keely the once-over, then made eye contact with Lane. "Mornin'."

"Two coffees and one mochaccino to go, please," Lane said.

"Good timing. Just made a fresh pot," Jen said over her shoulder.

They were outside sipping their coffees three minutes later.

"You're right, it's great coffee." Keely smiled.

"We'll go in for breakfast some day." Lane closed his eyes and felt the morning sun on his face.

"Deal." Keely hesitated. "My parents got another letter."

Lane stopped, holding the mochaccino in one hand and the coffee in the other. "What did it say?"

"It suggested they start saving for their daughter's funeral." Keely started walking east. "My mom is freaking."

"And your dad?"

"I'm afraid of what he might do. When it comes to his kids, he takes threats really seriously." Kelly looked toward the glass and blue metal of City Hall as they waited for the green light.

"What do you think?" Lane stood beside her and watched her reaction from the edge of his peripheral vision.

Keely shrugged. "I wonder why we just get threats and never any follow-through."

"Why warn the prey when you're planning an attack?" Lane asked.

"Exactly."

"You kept the letter?"

"Of course."

"Would you bring it in? I have someone who might be willing to take a close look at it."

"Okay." Keely stepped onto the street. They walked in silence back to the office. Lori was at her desk.

"Got something for you," Lori said as Lane set the mochaccino down in front of her. "Last year there was a guy from The Hague here for a convention. Gave a talk about prosecuting war criminals. Left his card. I phoned him and just caught him before he left his office. He works for the International Criminal Court. He's going to fax us copies of any documents he can find relating to either Borislav Goran or Andelko Branimir."

At six-thirty, Keely stood up from behind her desk and stretched. "No luck so far on a last name for Mladen."

"Maybe we should try checking out some street venues? The guy needs to make a living." Lane looked at his screen and the list of upcoming events. "Or we could hang out at Kensington and wait for Leo to turn up."

"Leo ever been arrested?" Keely asked.

"Don't know." Lane pointed at his screen. "There's something happening at Marda Loop on Friday night."

"Be nice to get out of here. The atmosphere is a bit chilly." Keely sat down and looked out over her computer.

Lane looked at Keely. She was still wearing her jacket. He looked sideways at her.

"I'm not talking temperature." Keely frowned at him.

"Oh. You mean the leper thing?" Lane asked.

"Leper?"

"You and I made Smoke look bad. Some of the guys around here are Smoke's boys. And I'm under investigation."

"For what?" Keely asked.

"I went out one night with a Glock and came back without it. Smoke disregarded the circumstances and ordered an investigation."

×

While listening to the grandfather clock ticking and Arthur snoring on the couch, Lane rubbed Roz behind the ears and thought about taking her for a walk.

Matt was at a movie and Christine was out with friends. *Just enjoy the quiet while it lasts,* Lane thought.

Arthur's snoring stopped and he sat up. "You think it'll be okay?"

"I do. I don't know why, I just know it will be all right. They caught the cancer early. We have a good doctor." Lane looked at Arthur.

The phone rang. Lane picked it up. "It's Keely."

Lane waited when he heard the tremor in her voice.

"There's a message painted on my garage door."

"Are you safe?" Lane asked.

"I think so. I don't want to call my parents. They're already upset enough. I'm sorry. I just didn't know who else to call."

"Give me your address," Lane said.

Twenty-five minutes later, he was there.

Keely lived in a condo on the western edge of the city. All the homes were two stories and had either one- or two-car garages. Fresh sod lay out front of 423. RAT was scrawled in red on the garage door. Lane parked across the street.

"I'm sorry." Keely had the door open before Lane could press the doorbell. She was wearing jeans and a T-shirt. Her red hair was down around her shoulders.

"Don't be sorry." Lane looked to his left at the garage door. "Any other messages?"

Keely shook her head. "It's an escalation. It was letters and phone calls before."

Lane walked to the garage door to take a closer look. The T on RAT had a tail that curled down to the right hand corner of the door. "Not very original."

Keely had her arms crossed under her breasts. "That's what I thought."

"Did you give the restaurant owner your address or phone number when you worked there?"

"No. Both were bogus." Keely went back to the front door. "Want a coffee?"

"Okay." Lane followed her inside, took off his shoes, and walked down the hallway to the kitchen and living room. The floors were the same maple as the cabinets. The blinds were open, and the window looked out to trees and blue sky. "Nice view." He looked at the law books on the coffee table and the picture of Keely with a blond-haired young man.

"We like it." She turned to Lane after pouring water into the coffee machine. "His name is Dylan. He's finishing his last year of law school." Keely closed the top of the coffee maker and switched it on. She sat on the loveseat across from Lane and put her feet on the coffee table. "Dylan's on his way. He was getting some stuff set up at the university."

"Have you got the letters?" Lane asked.

"In an envelope on the kitchen table." Keely looked over Lane's shoulder and into the kitchen.

"I'd like to get forensics to look at your garage door and the letters you've received thus far." Lane smelled coffee brewing and closed his eyes.

"Thus far?" Keely sat up.

"Do you think he'll quit?" Lane asked.

Keely shook her head, got up, and went to pour two cups of coffee. "Cream and sugar, right?"

"Please." Lane watched as she set the cup down in front of him. "Thanks."

"No problem." Keely sat down. "I didn't want to tell my dad. Things are pretty strained between us."

Lane waited.

"Ever since I moved in with Dylan, it's like my dad's disappointed in me. Nothing's ever said. I guess that's the problem; we don't talk. We used to be really close, but now he avoids me."

"Families are complicated." Lane looked at his coffee.

"I hear you've got kids."

"A niece and a nephew. Both came with baggage." *Keely's easy to talk to.*

"What kind of baggage?" Keely cradled her cup and sat back.

"Christine is my niece. She was rejected by her mother and escaped a polygamist community. My nephew Matt lost his mom to cancer. His dad started a new family. Matt was excess baggage as far as his dad was concerned. Now Matt's having to be the rock in the family while the rest of us spin out of control."

"Lori told me about Arthur. When is the operation?"

"We visit the surgeon. Then we find out."

Keely shrugged. "What about you? How come you're spinning out of control?"

Change the subject. "You didn't give your address or phone to the manager of the restaurant when you were undercover. But the person who painted your garage door also knows where your parents live. And I'm assuming all of your addresses are unlisted?"

Keely nodded.

"Then there's another avenue to consider." Lane set his coffee down.

"What's that?"

"The person responsible is probably a police officer with access to your personal information."

chapter 8

"Dr. Weaver?" Lane was on the phone at his desk at six o'clock the next morning. He had been prepared for an answering machine, but wasn't surprised when Fibre answered.

"Yes."

"My new partner is being threatened. This time the threat was painted on her garage door. She's received a series of threatening letters. Will you look into it?" Lane thought, *This isn't exactly part of Fibre's job description, but it's worth a try.*

"Of course. What's her address?"

Lane gave Fibre the address and hung up. *Why does he sound grateful? Ever since he dropped the N-bomb on Christine, he's been trying to make it up to me.*

He walked down the hallway to the fax machine. He fingered through the waiting documents and found twenty-six pages waiting for him. As he walked back to his desk, he saw that the name Borislav Goran figured prominently on each page.

Two hours later, Lane had the names and events mapped out on his computer. Corresponding images were added as visual reminders. Events and people were connected with arrows.

"Good morning." Keely put a cup of coffee on his desk. She sat down at her desk and sipped her cup. "Thanks for sending Dr. Weaver over. Odd character, that one. When I left, Dylan was trying to start up a conversation — without much success."

"That's Fibre for you. Great with the dead. Hopeless with the living. Thanks for the coffee, by the way." Lane took a taste. "Perfect."

Lori stood at the door to their office. She held a cup of tea in her hand. "Who do I thank for this?"

Lane pointed at Keely. "You're easy to train," Lori smiled.

Keely tilted her head to one side to see what Lane was working on. "The faxes came in this morning," he said.

"Then I'd better let you get to work." Lori left.

"What do you want me to do?" Keely asked.

"Take a look at these faxes, see what you can make of them. Add another perspective. How long do you think you'll need?"

Keely flipped through the pages. "An hour, or maybe a bit more."

"Can we meet at nine o'clock then?" Lane stood up. "I've got an appointment at eleven."

Gregory appeared in the doorway with his hands raised, palms pushed against either side of the doorframe. "Taking time off again, I see."

"That's right." Lane crossed his arms and waited for the staff sergeant to finish.

Keely sighed.

Gregory looked at her and nodded in Lane's direction. "Don't learn any bad habits from this one. He won't be around for long."

×

"I was hoping you'd return." Dr. Alexandre handed Lane a cup of coffee and sat across from him at the round table.

Lane set the coffee down and looked around the room. There were certificates on the wall and plants thirsty for water. He looked over the fresh cut flowers on the table. "You didn't think I'd show?"

"No." Dr. Alexandre waited for Lane's reaction.

It's odd being analyzed instead of doing the analysis. "What kind of coffee is this?" Lane asked.

"Trade secret," the doctor said.

"Perked?"

The doctor nodded. "Your powers of observation are not in question here."

"I'm not sure what you mean," Lane said.

"Yes you do."

Lane hesitated. He'd heard the "Let's cut through the bullshit" tone in her voice.

"If you want to ask, then ask. Let's get it out of the way," the doctor said.

She trusts you. She's not judging you. Maybe you should give her the same courtesy. "When did you have reassignment surgery?"

"Fourteen years ago."

"You don't mind being asked?"

"No. Do you mind being asked about being gay?" The doctor took a sip of coffee and waited.

Loraine said you could trust her. That's all you really need to know. Except maybe that you're not going to get out of this black hole on your own. "Depends on who's doing the asking."

"Yesterday, you spoke of being locked out of your family home," Alexandre said.

"Yes."

Alexandre leaned over to put her coffee down. Again, Lane spotted the doctor's Adam's apple as the collar of her blue sleeveless top fell forward. *I'm glad that's out of the way.* "Last night I had a nightmare. I used to have them quite a bit after what happened when I was thirteen." Lane sat back and studied the doctor. Alexandre was still, her face a mask.

What the hell — if she wants to know, I'll tell her. "It was a Sunday afternoon. A church picnic. My parents were talking with friends. My brother and I were down by the river bank throwing rocks into the water."

"Your brother's name?" the doctor asked.

"Joseph." Lane looked out the window, remembering the

details of that day. "It was windy. I threw a rock into the water. The wind carried the splash back at us and Joseph got most of it. He started yelling at me. Calling me a queer, a freak. Then he lunged at me to shove me into the river. I stepped to one side. Joseph lost his balance and fell into the water. The river was running fast, and it swept him downstream. I started screaming for help and running down the trail along the bank. Joseph never could swim very well. He was splashing around, trying to keep his head above water. He hit a rock or something and went under." Lane closed his eyes so that he could see it. "I ran down ahead of him. There was a branch leaning out into the water. I got into the river, held onto the branch, and grabbed Joseph by the arm. He was panicking and punched me in the face. I just held on until help came to pull us both onto shore."

"What was it like, after?"

You've got a knack for cutting to the heart of it all. "At first, it was exhilarating because we were alive. Then my mother asked what happened."

"Well?"

Lane looked back at Alexandre. Alexandre waited.

"In front of everyone, Joseph accused me of pushing him into the river. My father punched me in the side of the head. They took me home in disgrace. No good deed goes unpunished." Lane felt his voice wavering. *That's odd. I haven't felt much of anything in the past two months. Now I'm feeling what I felt that day.*

"Did any recent events cause this memory to resurface?" Dr. Alexandre asked.

"My father died recently. Joseph and his wife Margaret want to make a deal so I won't contest the will."

"Really?"

"I told them that unless they make provisions for Christine and Matt's education, I'll get a lawyer." Lane shook his head.

"Christine and Matt are your niece and nephew?"

"That's right." Lane looked at his watch.

"Could we meet again?" Alexandre wrote on the back of her business card.

Lane nodded.

"Before then, I want you to think about what else might have triggered the memory of your brother in the river." Alexandre handed Lane the business card with the appointment scrawled on the back.

×

Keely sat at the head of the conference table and sat Lane just around the corner. The faxed pages were fanned out in front of them. Lane looked at the printed copy of his map of names and events.

Keely sat behind her laptop. "Well, it looks like we might have Mladen's last name."

"Nezil. His name is on several of the documents." Lane pointed at an oval on his diagram.

"Didn't you have trouble reading some of these first-hand accounts?" Keely watched for Lane's reaction.

"You mean the execution of Mladen's brother, uncle, and father? The rapes of his mother and sister?"

"Yes."

"That wasn't what was especially disturbing."

"What was so disturbing, then?" Keely tried unsuccessfully to hide the sarcasm in her voice.

Lane took a breath and let the automatic angry reaction to sarcasm fade from his eyes and voice before he answered. "This part." Lane pointed at a quote he'd highlighted on one of the faxes and read it. "The militia took a break, drank some plum brandy, and a few even napped after they returned from executing the men. Then they were ordered by Borislav Goran to systematically rape the females and a handful of the boys."

Keely stared at her computer screen.

"It's so cold-blooded," Lane said. "It was like the militia treated murder and rape as if it was a job that included a necessary coffee break. That's what was particularly disturbing for me."

"I'm sorry. It's just that I've never seen anything like this before." Keely tried to smile and failed.

"If Goran is the name of the dead man we found, and if this is the same Mladen who watched what happened to his family, it certainly appears to be a motive for murder."

"His mother was so badly beaten during the rape that she died within hours. Mladen ended up in a refugee camp. It doesn't say what happened to his sister." Keely pointed at her screen.

"And it doesn't explain how Mladen ended up in Spain or how he lost his leg." Lane looked for his coffee, checked the inside of the empty cup, and tossed it in the garbage.

"There's something else here that I wonder about." Keely looked at Lane's map to see if he'd noticed it as well.

"What's that?"

"There was a female who was a member of the militia. She guarded the women and children of Mladen's village while the militiamen drank and slept. Witnesses describe her as a sniper. They also say she was Goran's wife."

"You think it's important?" Lane asked.

"Might be. I haven't met Jelena yet, but if Goran changed his identity to get into Canada, Jelena could have done the same."

This is getting muddier instead of clearer. "I don't know."

"It's a possibility."

"You're right, of course, but. . ."

Keely stared at him. "What?"

"Mladen has a motive."

"I still think we need to check out the woman." Keely frowned and crossed her arms under her breasts.

"I was hoping for answers and all we've got is more questions," Lane said. "So we need to talk with Jelena again, and we need to find out if this last name will help us find Mladen."

"I wanted to thank for coming over to my place," Keely said. "Things went well with my parents after you left."

"Your dad's talking to you?" Lane asked.

Keely smiled. "Dylan phoned my mom to tell her what happened. My dad phoned to see if I was okay. Then he came over, and we started to talk." She wiped her eyes.

"Good."

×

They stood in the shade of a pair of towering evergreens on either side of the bungalow's front sidewalk. The house had a fresh coat of green paint on its stuccoed exterior. It was one of a trio of meticulously manicured homes in Little Italy, a neighbourhood just north of the Calgary Zoo that had become trendy as people with money sought out homes closer to the city's core. Lane knocked on the door while Keely stood one step lower.

There was an intermittent thump as someone approached the front door along what sounded like a long hallway. The door opened to reveal Leo, in a pair of sweatpants, leaning on his crutch. His bare shoulders were broad and his arms were knotted with muscle. Leo smirked, revealing a mouthful of perfect teeth. "Been expecting you. Come in."

Lane and Keely followed Leo down the hallway to the kitchen at the back of the house.

Leo leaned on his crutch near the sink, opened the tap, and filled the coffee maker with water. "Want a cup?"

"Please," Lane said.

Keely lifted her eyebrows, creating several creases in her forehead. Lane shrugged and sat at the kitchen table. Keely hesitated.

Leo finished with the coffee machine and turned. "What happened to the other guy?"

"Other guy?" Lane asked.

"You know, your partner. The guy with the mustache." Leo pulled out a chair and leaned his crutch against the wall. He reached for a black T-shirt on the back of the chair, put it on, and sat.

"Detective Saliba is my partner now." Lane felt Keely's eyes on him.

"Take a load off, Saliba." Leo pulled out another chair. Keely sat.

Okay, Lane thought, *Let's get to the point.* "We're looking for Mladen Nezil. This is his last known address."

"Of course you are." Leo hooked one arm over the back of his chair. "Mladen lived here for over a year."

Get as much information as possible before asking for Mladen's new address. "I think I know why he reacted the way he did when I asked about Borislav Goran."

"Okay." Leo stopped smiling. He appeared to be sending a challenge to Lane.

"Goran ordered the massacre." *Let's see how much he knows.*

"The murders. The rapes. Mladen and his sister were the only members of their family to survive that one." Leo got up when he heard the coffee maker splutter. Lane gathered three cups from the counter. Leo poured.

After he sat down, Leo said, "Mladen told me to tell it all to you. Answer all your questions."

"How come he's not here to answer them himself?" Keely asked.

"He saved up enough to buy his own place. Moved there a couple of weeks ago." Leo watched the detectives' reactions.

"What happened to Mladen's surviving sister?" Keely asked.

Nice move.

"She was killed by a mortar. Mladen and his sister traveled to the Canadian headquarters in that area. The Canadians were there on a peacekeeping mission. Mladen and Zara were talking to the soldiers outside the building. The Canadians were behind a sandbag wall. A mortar round dropped on them. It decapitated Zara. A surgeon amputated Mladen's leg. The Canadians had a kind of operating theatre set up in the car park under their headquarters. When Mladen was well enough, he was transported to Spain, where he went to school and applied to come to Canada." Leo took a sip of coffee.

"Where does he live now?" Lane asked. *I wonder if he'll tell us.*

"First, you need to know this: Mladen still has nightmares about what happened to his family and to him. The soldiers raped him as well as his sister. He came to this country to start fresh and now the past has caught up to him in a particularly horrible way. There's a fragile strength to the guy. He looks like he's healthy, but the scars left by what happened to his family open up at the most unexpected times."

Lane waited.

"Will you treat him with dignity?" Leo asked.

Lane nodded.

"He might not be home. He works two jobs. We've got a gig on Friday night at Marda Loop." Leo grabbed a piece of paper and began to write. "This is Mladen's address and phone."

Keely took the paper and handed it to Lane.

"What time's the performance on Friday?" Lane asked.

"Eight." Leo stood up and reached for his crutch. "I need to get to work."

×

Lane and Keely sat in the sub shop, ate their sandwiches, and drank their coffee while watching the comings and goings across the parking lot at Jelena's Alterations.

Keely wiped her mouth with a napkin. She glanced at Jordan, who was creating sandwiches behind the glass. "When do you want to go and talk with her?"

"She'll come over here for a coffee and a smoke. I'd like to question her away from her shop. Besides, that'll give you more time to check Jordan out."

Keely blushed and looked out the window as if to prove she hadn't noticed Jordan's romance-novel good looks. "Here she comes."

Jelena blew smoke into the air as she puffed her way across the parking lot. When she got closer, Lane and Keely could see a furious faraway look about her. She set the half-smoked cigarette in an ashtray on the picnic table outside, opened the door to Jordan's sub shop and walked past the detectives without noticing them.

"Coffee?" Jordan asked.

Jelena nodded.

"Lunch?" Jordan asked.

Jelena shook her head. She held out a five-dollar bill.

"You can't live on cigarettes." Jordan smiled as he handed her a coffee and took the five. He looked over her shoulder in the direction of the detectives.

"You'd be surprised at what you can live on." Jelena appeared to miss Jordan's warning glance. "When I was in the war, I lived on cigarettes and plum brandy for two weeks. We called them field rations."

"There's someone here to see you," Jordan said.

Jelena stood perfectly still. Lane watched as she studied their reflections in the display glass before putting a lid on her coffee and turning to face them.

"More questions?" Jelena asked.

"Yes."

Lane stood, wrapped what remained of his sandwich, picked up his coffee, and held the door open. Jelena walked past him and sat at the picnic table. Lane and Keely sat across from her. Jelena filled her lungs with tobacco and looked at Keely. "Who's this?"

"Detective Saliba," Lane said.

Jelena studied Keely with a mixture of hatred and fear. Then she turned to Lane, acting as if Keely didn't exist.

"We have some questions about Borislav Goran," Keely said.

Jelena pretended not to hear the question. *No matter what you do, you'll offend one of them, so go with your gut.* "Tell us about Goran."

"He was a cousin of my husband, as I told you before. Borislav was in the militia during the war. He was killed near the end." Jelena took a sip of coffee, then butted out her cigarette. She reached into the side pocket of her jacket to get another.

"You saw him die?" Lane asked.

Jelena nodded while lighting another cigarette. "He was hit by an artillery shell. Not much left to identify."

"*Very* convenient," Keely said.

Jelena blinked but gave no other indication she'd heard the remark.

"Borislav Goran is named in a series of war crimes. Do you have any knowledge of these crimes?" Lane asked.

"What have these questions got to do with Andelko?"

"Your husband was in the militia with Goran." Lane made it sound like fact.

She smiled. "Lots of people were in the militia."

"You saw Borislav die, so you were in the militia as well," Keely said.

Lane heard the anger in Keely's voice. Felt the tension between the two women.

"It was war. One survives in war." Jelena put the cigarette to her lips and allowed a lazy wisp of smoke to rise into the summer air.

"Was your husband a war criminal?" Lane asked.

She exhaled. "No."

"Were you a war criminal?"

"No."

"Were you and Andelko married during the war?" Lane asked.

"No." Jelena looked at the ash on the end of her cigarette and stubbed it into the ashtray. "Have you ever been in a war?"

"No," Lane said.

Jelena stood, reaching for her coffee. "Then you have no idea what it is like. Have you found the juggler yet?"

"Not yet."

"He wanted to kill Andelko."

With that, Jelena walked away. Lane and Keely watched her cross the parking lot and open the door to her shop.

"She acted like you didn't exist. Is it because your name sounds like it might be Muslim?" Lane asked.

Keely frowned and nodded. "Probably. I wondered if you noticed."

"We know that Mladen's family was Muslim."

"Yes they were."

"And many Muslims were ethnically cleansed."

"That's right." Keely watched a pickup truck as it slowed to bounce over a speed bump.

"So now we have to find out more about Jelena Branimir and Mladen Nezil. Want to take a drive past Mladen's place?"

It took less than half an hour to find the bungalow on the east side of town. Lane knocked on the front door, and Keely tried the back. No one was home.

"How is Keely working out?" Arthur asked.

Lane sat at the kitchen table while Arthur put the finishing touches on supper. "She's got a mind of her own. And it looks like she's smart."

"Sounds pretty good to me." Arthur put the salad on the table.

"And as stubborn as she is smart." Lane picked a tomato from the salad.

Arthur chuckled. "That could make things interesting."

"It already has. First there wasn't enough information. Now there's too much. On top of that, someone is threatening her. It looks like it's either a guy with connections to a group of bikers or someone inside the police force."

Arthur turned his head as he washed his hands in the sink. "What makes you think it's from the inside?"

"Access to her personal information." Lane picked out a slice of cucumber. Roz licked Lane's feet.

"Is this dangerous or just messy?"

Lane considered the question. "Probably both. Where are the kids?" He looked down at the dog. Roz looked up at Lane, then continued licking the salt from his ankle.

"Matt's asleep downstairs, and as for Christine. . ." Arthur shrugged.

"So it's just you and me?" Lane smiled.

Arthur put on the oven mitts and pulled chicken from the oven. The scent of butter and thyme filled the kitchen.

"Smells great," Lane said.

"I've decided I want a double mastectomy," Arthur said.

Lane waited.

"If I get both done at the same time, I won't have to worry about going back to have the other done in the future. And I won't have to go through the whole thing again if they don't get all of the tumour the first time." Arthur looked directly at Lane.

Lane turned as he heard the front door open.

"Come on in," Christine called.

Lane stood. Arthur placed the chicken on a hot plate in the middle of the kitchen table.

"This is Daniel," said Christine, nodding toward the young man whose hand she was holding. "Can he stay for supper?"

"Hello." Daniel tried to smile. He was dark-haired and stood a head taller than Christine. He looked at Lane, then Arthur, then back at Lane. "It's kind of short notice."

Lane saw the bruise on the right side of Daniel's chin. And he saw intimacy in the way Christine looked at him.

"We've got lots." Arthur poked Lane in the ribs and said, "Be sociable."

"Would you like a beer?" Lane asked.

"Aren't you going to ask him to *sit down* first?" Christine asked.

Lane reacted to the sarcasm in Christine's voice. "Daniel, would you like to come in and have a beer before dinner, during dinner, after dinner, or any one or all of the above?" *Why are you giving him such a hard time?*

"Maybe this wasn't such a good idea." Daniel turned to leave.

"Oh, just ignore him. Meet my other uncle." Christine glared at Lane as she guided Daniel across the kitchen.

Lane felt an unaccountable rage grab hold and shake him. He stood up, turned to sit down, changed his mind, walked to the front door, stuffed his feet into his shoes, picked up Roz's leash, and shook it. Roz scampered from the kitchen and danced in circles around Lane. He grabbed her by the collar and hooked her to the leash. Within forty-five seconds, they were out the door and fifty metres down the sidewalk.

Roz trotted to keep up as Lane strode uphill — always uphill. *Christine! You treat me like shit! And why are you always after the guys who will treat you the same way?* The same questions ran through Lane's mind. He walked uphill until he arrived on the spine of a ridge overlooking downtown.

The urban forest made all but the tallest buildings in the downtown core invisible. He looked at Roz, who lay panting in a patch of shade.

Ninety minutes later, Lane let Roz into the backyard.

Arthur opened the back door. "Explain."

"Where are they?" Lane shut the gate behind him. Roz lapped up water from her bowl on the deck.

"They went to a movie." Arthur went back into the house. Lane sat down under the umbrella. Arthur reappeared with a plate of salad and chicken. He set it on the table. "Daniel insisted that we fill a plate for you and save it for your return. What do you want to drink?"

"A beer."

"Get it yourself. And while you're at it get me one too." Arthur sat down.

Lane took off his shoes and walked barefoot into the kitchen. As he reached for the beer, he heard Matt snoring downstairs.

Outside, he handed Arthur a beer and a glass before sitting down and pouring one for himself. He looked at the salad and inhaled the scent of balsamic vinegar, oregano, and feta cheese. After a sip of beer, he picked up a fork, and tasted the salad.

"Explain," Arthur said.

"I can't. They walked in, I saw the bruise on his face, saw the way she looked at him, and reacted to her sarcasm. I don't know why she keeps getting involved with guys who treat her like that."

"Like what?" Arthur rested his beer on the top of his belly.

Why is he being so calm about this? He's the one who usually reacts emotionally. He felt as if his teeth were about to clamp down on his tongue. "She has a history of picking guys who aren't good to her. You know. The kind of guy we met at emergency. The one who gave her a black eye."

"Daniel got the bruise on his face from the same guy who gave Christine the bruise. In fact, Daniel drove her home after he got into the middle of the fight to protect her. Daniel was trying to stop Christine from being hit again." Arthur waited for Lane's reaction.

Lane looked at the bubbles rising in the amber of his beer. "Shit."

"Exactly."

Lane picked up his fork and put it down again. "I apologize."

"It's not me you need to apologize to. But I'll accept anyway after the way you've shut me out lately." Arthur lifted his glass and took a drink. "And quit pretending it's all about the way Christine treats you. It's more than just that, and you know it."

chapter 9

"Is Christine around?" Lane checked his email as he talked on the phone.

"She's at work," Arthur said, his tone implying that Lane should know her schedule.

"Of course. I'll have to talk to her when I get home," Lane said.

"If she's here."

"Yes." Lane hung up just as Lori stuck her head into his office.

"Got some information from the Department of National Defense." She held out a file with faxes inside.

"Mladen?" Lane took the folder.

"Yep. I took a quick peek. The kid's moved around. Some of the peacekeepers chipped in, pulled some strings, and got him into Spain for medical treatment, rehab, and schooling. After that, they helped him get over here."

"Thanks."

"Have a rough night?"

Lane looked at her but didn't answer.

Keely walked in and sat down at the desk next to Lane's. "Kids giving you a rough time?"

"My niece brought a boyfriend home for supper. He had a bruise on his chin, and I jumped to the wrong conclusion." Lane waited for their reactions.

Keely looked at Lori.

"How'd he get the bruise?" Lori asked.

"He stepped in when another guy hit Christine. The guy who hit her was drunk, and he hit Daniel as well."

"Daniel's the boyfriend?" Keely asked.

"Looks like it."

"So he tried to help Christine, and you thought he had been beating up on her?" Lori asked.

"Something like that," Lane said. *How did I end up in the middle of an interrogation?*

"Like what, exactly?" Keely asked.

"Well, I thought she was bringing home a guy who was bad news. She's been known to pick guys who aren't good for her."

"And you did what?" Lori asked.

"I got mad and left. Took the dog for a walk."

"And now you need to apologize, right?" Lori asked.

"That's right."

"What a dad." Keely smiled. "About the same thing my dad would have done under the circumstances. How about yours?" She looked at Lori.

"Sounds like something mine would do too." Lori began to laugh.

"What's so funny?" Lane asked.

"You are." Lori left.

"Let's get through this information on Mladen. Any luck contacting him yet?" Keely asked.

"Not yet. We may have to go to Marda Loop on Friday night to catch the show." *Friday's going to be a busy day.* Lane picked up the file. "Let's take a look at this."

They began skimming the pages.

"Here's something." Keely pointed at a paragraph on the second page. "There were other witnesses to the massacre. Five of them identified Borislav Goran as the one who ordered the executions. And thirty-seven bodies were discovered in a mass grave after the end of the war."

"That could easily mean that Jelena is right and Mladen had a motive." Lane held up another paragraph. "Apparently, Mladen was taken care of by a group of Canadian officers and enlisted men who managed to get him to Spain. Some members of the Canadian Embassy in Madrid helped get him enrolled in a school and arranged for medical care. This confirms that Mladen lost his entire family in the war."

"As you said, it gives him a pretty strong motive for killing Branimir." Keely looked at the computer screen. "Do you think we should swing by Mladen's place again?"

"Yes. And we should check into this: Borislav had a wife named Safina Goran. I wonder if there are any photographs?" Lane thought for a minute. "And I wonder if Lori's friend in The Hague can tell us anything about Andelko Branimir?"

"It's worth a try. I'll ask Lori."

They left fifteen minutes later, and after thirty more, they were parked in front of Mladen's west-facing bungalow. Lane looked across the valley. A railway line, a freeway, and a creek ran north and south. Further west was downtown, and further still were the mountains.

"Do you ever get tired of looking at them?" Keely looked at the edges where blue sky and grey peaks met.

"No." Lane watched a man cutting Mladen's grass. He wore a ballcap and chewed the end of a cigar while he worked. The man worked his way up near Mladen's doorstep, changed directions, looked up, and spotted the detectives parked at the sidewalk. The mower quit. The man took the cigar from his mouth. He reached up with his free hand and picked a piece of tobacco from his lower lip.

"We're looking for Mladen Nezil," Keely said.

"So?" The man took off his hat and wiped the inside elbow of his shirtsleeve across his shining scalp.

Try something different. He got out of the car, walked forward, and offered his hand. "Detective Lane."

"Harvey." He shook Lane's hand. Lane felt calluses that must have built up over a quarter-century of labour.

"Good strong grip," Harvey said. "Never trust a man with a sissy handshake."

Lane opened his mouth, closed it, and opened it again. "He's not home?"

"Nope. The guy works all day, then makes money as some kinda street performer. I was cuttin' my grass, so I just cut his too. Retired, so I got time on my hands." Harvey stuck the cigar back in his mouth.

"Know where he works?" Lane asked.

"Nope. All I know is the old owners were thrilled when Mladen paid cash for the place."

Keely asked, "What's he like?"

Harvey shrugged and pulled the cigar out with his right hand. "Don't see much of him. All he does is work and sleep."

"He doesn't own a car?" Lane asked.

Harvey looked at the detectives. He pointed at Keely with his cigar. "Kid's a hard worker. Doesn't bother anyone. Just trying to make a go of it. You're barkin' up the wrong tree with this one." He turned, went back to the mower, reached down, and started the motor, destroying the temporary quiet.

"Guess that means we can go," Keely said.

✕

"It's okay. I understand. You apologized. It's all good. My father acted much the same way when he met my sister's fiancé for the first time." Daniel sat with his legs splayed out in front of him. He leaned against the back door as he sat on the back step. He shifted his six-foot five-inch frame so he could lean his elbows onto his knees.

Lane caught himself watching Daniel's brown eyes like he would a suspect's.

"It's not okay as far as I'm concerned." Christine tapped the table with her middle finger to emphasize her point. "You never stopped to find out the facts. Your job is all about gathering evidence and discovering the facts. You never gave me a chance to explain — you just reacted emotionally."

Matt covered his mouth. Christine glared at him.

Arthur looked over his glasses at her. "Did you just say something about reacting emotionally?"

Christine smiled. Arthur looked at Lane. Daniel laughed. The phone rang.

Lane got up, put his hand on Daniel's shoulder as he eased by, and went into the kitchen. Less than a minute later, he poked his head out the door. "I have to go."

×

"I was just opening the front door to go outside. There was an explosion. I think it was a pipe bomb." Keely's red hair hung down to her shoulders, framing her face.

A redheaded officer from the bomb disposal unit held the remains of the explosive device in his palms so Lane and Keely could see them. "This is what we've found so far. Not very sophisticated but still lethal. Either someone was just trying to scare the hell out of you, or this thing went off early."

Lane read the name SHANE on the officer's uniform.

Keely looked at the burned-out remains of her car. "So it was taped to the bottom of my gas tank?"

"We found some duct tape," Shane said, "so that's our working theory."

A tow truck driver crawled under the front bumper of Keely's car and attached a cable. Firemen packed up their equipment. The pavement was wet and shimmering. Lane looked across the street as a photographer with a long lens took their picture. "Maybe we should go inside."

Keely's condominium had one bedroom with a kitchen and living room divided by a nook.

"You want a cold drink?" Keely reached into the fridge.

"Water sounds good." Lane sat on the couch. Keely handed him a bottle of water and sat at the other end.

Someone knocked at the door. Startled, Keely spilled her water onto the carpet.

Lane got up. "I'll get it." He reached for the doorknob. "Who are you expecting?"

"Dylan. My parents." Keely put her bottle, with what little water was left in it, on the coffee table.

Lane opened the door to face a round, dark-haired man and a taller, red-haired woman. Both of them appeared ready for a scrap.

"Who are you?" the woman asked.

"Yes, where is my daughter?" The man put his fists on his hips while looking Lane up and down.

"Mom. Dad. This is Detective Lane. My new partner. I called him right after I called you and Dylan." Keely stood behind her partner. "Lane. This is my father Amir and my mother Katherine."

Lane smiled, remembering his own defensive reaction after meeting Daniel for the first time. He offered his hand to shake Amir's.

Katherine brushed past the two of them to hug her daughter. "You sure you're okay?" Mother and daughter sat on the couch.

"Fine, mom."

"What's being done to protect our daughter?" Amir asked.

"Your daughter needs you now, Amir. Get over here," Katherine said.

Amir glanced at his wife and sat down beside his daughter. He put his arm around Keely. She began to sob. Katherine started crying right after Amir did.

Lane was looking for a box of tissues when the door opened. The man entering was just under six feet, with sandy hair, and carried a briefcase. He held a key as he walked into the room. He stood open-mouthed at the scene on the couch.

"Let me take that, Dylan," Lane said.

Dylan handed over his briefcase and keys, went to the couch, knelt down, and soon found himself in the middle of a group hug. Katherine leaned against the arm of the couch, smiled at the scene, then looked at Lane. Lane handed her a tissue.

"Thanks." She wiped her eyes and blew her nose.

Lane waited five minutes before asking, "How about some pizza?"

Forty-five minutes later, they arrived at Lane's house — just ten minutes before the pizza deliveryman. Arthur set the pizzas out on the table on the deck, poured wine, and worked his way through the introductions.

"You speak Arabic?" Amir asked.

"Of course." Arthur proved his point by speaking in the tongue of his father and mother.

"They'll be busy for a while," Keely said to Lane.

Lane stood up. "I need to make a few calls," he said before exiting into the kitchen.

Christine nodded in Amir's direction. "Does he know?" she asked Keely.

"Know what?"

"About our uncles?" Christine glanced to see if Amir had overheard, but he was happily talking with Arthur.

"That they've been very kind to our daughter and to us?" Katherine asked.

"That he's my *partner*?"

Christine rolled her eyes. "You know what I mean. Do you have a problem with it?"

"Do you?" Keely glanced at her mother.

Christine's face went red; she opened her mouth as if to respond, closed it, and frowned.

Lane came back outside. He looked at Keely and Dylan.

"You know you can't go home until we find out who this bomber is?"

"What?" Dylan looked at Keely.

"A safe house has been arranged for you. I'd recommend that Katherine and Amir stay there as well. Does your brother live in town?"

"Yes, but you don't have to worry about Amir," Keely said.

"I'm wondering how the bomber got your address?" Lane asked.

Keely shook her head. "You think it's someone from work?"

"It's more than a distinct possibility," Lane said, then wondered, *How come she believes her brother is safe?*

chapter 10

Bomb Misses Its Target

A bomb destroyed a vehicle owned by a detective with the Calgary Police Service last night.

"We are in the initial stages of the investigation," Staff Sergeant Barton explained. "It appears that the device was attached to the underside of the vehicle."

A source within the police force said that the bomb might have been meant to warn the detective, who worked undercover to expose the illegal activities of the owner and patrons of a local restaurant.

×

"Fibre has some information for us. It's time you and I sat down with him." Lane handed Keely a coffee.

"Those Nanaimo bars look tasty." Keely leaned closer to the glass display case.

"Before I forget, Christine asked me to tell you 'Not anymore.' Don't know what it means, but there you are." Lane stepped outside the door, took a sip of coffee, and felt the morning sun on his face.

Keely stepped past him. "You're happy this morning."

She's right! "Yes I am, and so are you."

"I slept right through last night. Didn't realize how stressed I was." She walked over to the car. "My dad and Dylan started to talk last night. That was a relief."

Lane held up the keys. "You want to drive?"

She smiled. "Sure. Where to?"

"The hospital." *Looks like I'm going to be there every day for the next little while.*

Ten minutes later, they had parked in the lot in front of Fibre's glass and brick building. Keely followed Lane to the elevator. Inside she asked, "How do I approach him? Fibre has a bit of a reputation."

Lane looked at her. "I'm not sure. Do what you think needs to be done, I guess."

He knocked on the door to Dr. Weaver's office and opened it. Weaver looked up as they came in. "It was rumoured you were working with a new partner."

"Keely Saliba, Dr. Weaver." Lane stepped to one side so that Keely could stand next to him. Weaver remained seated, nodded, and used his hand to indicate they should sit down.

"Colin?" Lane asked. Fibre looked up.

Use no judgment in your voice. He just doesn't know what to do about you or with you, has trouble expressing emotion, and he has no clue what to do in social situations. "It's polite to shake the hand of my partner when you meet her for the first time."

"Of course. My apologies." Fibre reached across his desk. Lane noted the reflection of the doctor's Rolex on the desktop.

"Good to meet you." Keely shook Fibre's hand and smiled.

"There is some information to share with you." Fibre looked at Keely. "With both of you."

"Is it about the threats aimed at Keely?" Lane asked.

"Partly. The printer used for at least one of the letters is consistent with printers used by the police service. However, no DNA or fingerprints were found on the letters or the envelopes. We are working to find out if there was any evidence left on the components of the pipe bomb or on Ms. Saliba's car. By the way, did you see your photograph in this morning's paper? Both of you are quite photogenic." Dr. Weaver looked at Lane. "We did have more success with the reconstruction of the face of Andelko Branimir." He leaned over and clicked an icon on his computer. He turned the screen so that Lane and Keely could see the images.

"There are many similarities between the unique features of the victim's skull and the pictures on both sets of identification. Also. . ." Fibre created an outline of the skull's features and dragged it onto the photo from Andelko Branimir's driver's license. "When I superimpose either of the photographs on the outline, they match. There is a very high probability that the skull, Branimir, and Goran are all one and the same."

"It confirms what we've suspected so far," Keely said.

"An accurate supposition," Fibre said.

Let's get back to the matter at hand. "So the person who has been sending the threatening notes and who planted the pipe bomb has been careful to leave no evidence behind?" Lane asked.

"Very." Fibre turned the computer screen back around.

Lane got up. "In a way, that supports my theory that it's someone from the department who has at least some knowledge of how evidence is gathered."

"There is one other thing," Fibre said, reaching inside his desk and pulling out a small paper envelope. He opened the top and eased its contents onto his desktop. "This was found in a pocket of the leather jacket that was with the Branimir remains." A silver spider pin lay on the glass tabletop. It was the approximate size of a loonie. Fibre used a pair of tweezers from his drawer to turn the insignia over. The word TARANTULA was engraved on the back. "It took some time to clean it up, but this was what we discovered."

Keely said, "The Tarantulas. That's what Goran's unit called itself."

Lane smiled at the doctor. "As usual, Colin, you've helped us with some solid evidence."

Fibre turned red from cheeks to forehead. "We'll keep working on the remains of the pipe bomb to see if there was any evidence left behind."

×

Lane sat next to Arthur in the waiting room. Half a grey wall separated them from the hallway. Two hours ago, the waiting room had been overflowing. Now the only other people remaining were two women who sat side by side staring at a poster of flowers on the wall.

"Let me do the talking," Arthur said.

"Yes." *That must be the tenth time you've said that in the last hour.*

A nurse appeared. She was blonde, tall, and broad-shouldered. She pointed at the pair of women. "Your turn."

She has a very soothing voice. "We're next, then," he said.

Arthur sighed. "When this is all over, could we go on a holiday?"

"Where?"

"Somewhere where the food is fabulous, the view is amazing, and we can put our feet up or go shopping, depending on the day." Arthur put his hand on Lane's.

"With or without kids?" Lane asked.

Arthur looked at his partner. "Do you think they'd want to come with us?"

Lane shrugged. "We could ask them."

"We've never had a holiday with kids. It might be fun."

"Or it might be—"

"—a disaster."

They heard the squeak of approaching shoes. The nurse appeared. "Mr. Merali?"

"Yes." Arthur stood.

Lane followed them down the hall and into an examining room. The nurse held up a blue gown. "Change into this, please. It ties in the front. Dr. Dugay will be with you shortly." She closed the door and left them alone.

Arthur took off his shirt, and Lane hung it up. Arthur changed into the gown and sat on the examining table. The white paper cover crackled.

Lane sat down next to the door. Arthur looked at the wall.

There was a double tap at the door, and the surgeon strode in. Dr. Dugay was over six feet tall, had unruly sandy brown hair, and wore a white coat and a smile. He checked the file in his hand. "Mr. Merali?"

Arthur nodded. Dugay glanced at the file. He tapped a few keys on a computer keyboard, and an x-ray image of Arthur's chest appeared on a flat screen. "It's nearly in the middle of the breast, so that leaves us with some room for margins."

"Margins?" Arthur asked.

He's choking on the words.

"We usually use two-centimetre margins when we remove a tumour."

"Then?" Arthur began to cry.

"We do radiation and sometimes chemo, depending on what we find and what the biopsy results are. There are other factors as well."

Arthur wiped his eyes and looked at Lane. "You talk."

"Arthur would like a double mastectomy," Lane said.

Dugay turned, surprised to discover another person in the room. "Mr. . . . ?" The surgeon held out his hand.

Lane stood. "Lane. Arthur and I are partners. He may not be able to talk right now, so I may have to ask or answer any questions."

"Partners?" Dugay looked at Arthur.

Arthur nodded. Lane saw the doctor's eyes open a bit wider. "Oh."

He gets it now. Let's see what happens next.

"A double mastectomy is certainly one way to go," Dugay said.

"Arthur's sister died of breast cancer almost two years ago. With a family history like that, we'd prefer not to take any chances."

"I understand," Dugay said. "Do you want me to explain the options available?"

Arthur shook his head. "No."

"We went through all of the options with Arthur's sister," Lane said. "Right now, it's the waiting that's causing him the most anxiety. He's confident he's made the right choice. How soon will the surgery be?"

"If you like, as soon as next week. There has been a cancellation. We have an opening if it's not too soon."

Arthur wiped at his eyes. Lane waited for an indication from him. Arthur nodded.

"A week would be fine," Lane said.

×

"Is working late on a Friday night your idea of fun?" Lane asked.

Keely stood next to him, watching the crowd through binoculars. From the parking lot, they could look down on the road and the crowd. Thirty-Third Avenue was blocked at both ends by traffic barriers and patrol cars. The side streets were similarly closed off. The two sides of the road were lined with restaurants, retailers, and coffee shops. People gathered at the intersection or walked between display tables set up along one side of the street. A breeze billowed the tent fabric shading many of the tables. The setting sun made the colours richer, thicker.

Keely looked at her watch. "It's almost eight."

Both turned at the sound of a sassy trumpet announcing an arrival to their left. A figure on stilts walked into the intersection. The crowd looked up at the performer. The slick red fabric on one arm of the malabarista contrasted with the white fabric on the other. The colours met somewhere near the malabarista's navel. A magpie's nest of synthetic scarlet hair drew everyone's eyes to the performer's face.

"Mladen," Lane said.

"Leo's behind him," said Keely, still surveying the scene through her binoculars.

The music stopped. Leo, dressed in black, placed an equipment bag over a manhole cover at the centre of the intersection. He reached inside, pulled out three blue balls, and tossed them up one at a time to Mladen, who began to juggle. Leo started to play his trumpet again, moving around in a circle, gradually increasing the circumference, pushing the crowd back. That task complete, he went back to the bag and made a big deal about putting on surgical gloves. Mladen spread his feet, obscenely hung each ball between his legs, and dropped them one at a time. Leo caught them and placed them back in the bag. The crowd roared its approval.

Next, Leo pulled three shafts, each a metre long, from the bag. He attached glass globes on each end and turned the globes on. After all three objects were assembled, he held them up. The globes had minds of their own, randomly changing colour from red to green to white.

Mladen impatiently tapped his foot, and Leo tossed the batons up one at a time. Mladen twirled and flipped each into the air. As the sky darkened, the spinning globes became blurs of colour.

Leo picked up the trumpet and began to play a passionate Latin tune that had Mladen moving to its rhythm, the crowd clapping, and children pushing to the front so they could dance. Mladen tossed the batons to impossible heights, catching them only to throw them higher. Each time a baton flew into the air, it became a miniature fireworks wheel. Then, with a bounce, he launched the batons into the air, threw his arms up, flipped forward, tucked in his knees, rolled, and landed back on his stilts in time to catch the falling batons.

Leo changed tunes. Mladen performed a backflip, not noticing that a child had pushed his way out from the crowd into the performing area. Just as Mladen shifted his weight to his right leg, the toddler tripped, fell forward, and ran into Mladen's left leg. The child rolled behind him as Mladen's leg swung up like an empty swing.

The crowd held its breath as Mladen fought to remain upright. He flipped the three batons into the air, regained his balance, avoided the child, and caught the first two batons. The third was out of his grasp and exploded on the pavement.

Leo continued to play as Mladen turned, bent down, and looked at the boy. The crowd moved closer, blocking the detectives' view.

"What's he doing?" Lane asked.

"Can't see," Keely replied.

The crowd roared its approval and began to clap. They

were still clapping as Lane and Keely made their way down to the intersection and waited for the audience to disperse.

Part of the crowd gathered around Leo to drop money into his hat. When they finished, Leo cradled his hat and smiled up at Mladen, who was talking with a woman holding the boy who had tumbled into Mladen's leg.

Leo moved closer to Mladen, who leaned on the trumpeter's shoulder and undid one stilt before lifting the other and dropping to his good leg. He sat down and unstrapped the other leg.

"Thank you for being so understanding," the mother said.

"No problem." Mladen smiled, until he spotted the detectives.

The mother looked at the detectives. "Did you see that?"

"Only part of it," Keely said.

The woman shook her head. "You really missed something great! And all he was worried about was if my son was all right." She dropped a large bill into the hat and left the intersection.

Lane watched Leo and Mladen transfer the money from the overflowing hat into a bag. "A good night?" he asked.

Leo packed their gear, including the ruined baton, into the bag. Then he strapped the stilts to the outside of the bag. Mladen picked up bits of glass and dropped them into the palm of his left hand. "A very good night."

"We've been having trouble tracking you down," Keely said. "Could we take a minute to talk, please?"

Nice move, Lane thought.

Mladen hefted the bag with his right hand. He walked over to a nearby garbage can and dropped the bits of glass into it. Leo hung the trumpet from his neck and tucked his crutch under his armpit. Mladen looked at Lane and then at Keely. "I'm hungry."

They followed him to a nearby deli. They sat outside at

a picnic table. Mladen and Leo ordered Montreal smoked beef sandwiches.

"Coffee?" Lane turned to his partner.

"Water." Keely gave Lane an apologetic look. "I can't sleep if I drink coffee this late."

"They have the best Montreal smoked beef in the city." Mladen wiped the sweat from his forehead with the sleeve of his black T-shirt.

"How do you guys get around?" Lane asked.

"Bus, C-train, bike. Tonight we might splurge and take a taxi," Leo said.

"My neighbour said you talked to him," Mladen said.

"That's correct," Lane said.

"Ask your questions," Mladen said.

"When was the last time you saw Andelko Branimir or Borislav Goran?" Keely asked.

Mladen looked up as the waiter brought their drinks. The malabarista took a long pull on his soft drink. Leo opened his bottled water and tipped it back.

"I don't know this Andelko," Mladen said, "but when I was a boy, Goran came to my town with his militia. They called themselves Tarantulas."

"Did you know Borislav Goran before that?" Keely asked.

"He was a policeman before the war."

"When did you see Goran in Canada?"

Mladen shrugged. "Never."

"Did you see his wife, Safina Goran?"

"No." Mladen looked to his left. The waiter brought two plates with sandwiches, pickles, and coleslaw. Mladen picked up half of a sandwich and seemed to inhale it. In less than thirty seconds, he was licking his fingers and starting to work on the other half.

Lane sipped his coffee. *He appears to be telling the truth. Let him finish eating, then ask the question.*

Keely looked at Lane. He gave her a barely perceptible shake of his head, then turned sideways and watched the crowd thinning as the darkness deepened. He waited until he heard the sound of a straw sucking the bottom of an empty cup, then turned to face Mladen. "Why didn't you join?"

Mladen lifted his mouth from the straw. "Join?"

"The fighting."

Leo glared at Lane. Keely's eyes narrowed.

"Why didn't I become a murderer, you mean?"

Lane nodded. "That's correct. Why didn't you become a murderer?"

Mladen looked toward the dispersing crowd without seeing it. He set the cup down. Lane tucked his feet under his body and held onto the edge of the table, bracing himself in case Mladen reacted as he had last time.

Mladen focused on Lane. "Before she died, my mother told me. . ." He took a breath. "'Take care of your sister.' Then she grabbed my hand. I thought she was going to break my fingers. 'Promise me you won't become a monster like those men, like that Goran,' she said. After she died, we buried our mother. Then my sister and I left our town and went to the city."

If he's lying, he's very good at it. "How can we get in touch with you if we need to?"

Mladen gave them his phone number at work. "I get home late every night," he said. "In the summer, Leo and I make our money at the Stampede and festivals like this one. This is our busy time."

Ten minutes later, Lane and Keely were driving down Fourteenth Street hill to where it bottomed out and crossed Seventeenth Avenue. "I'd like to talk with Jelena again," Keely said. "And this time, could we talk to the daughter too?"

Lane thought for a moment. "Sunday might be the best time. Her business is open every other day. You want to set it up?"

Keely nodded. "Okay. And. . ."

"What?"

"I'd like to ask for a sample of the daughter's DNA."

"How come?"

"If Goran was the monster the evidence says he was, there may be another suspect."

chapter 11

Revelations from Bishop Paul About Former Police Chief Smoke

Bishop Paul has revealed some of the inner workings of a controversial local men's club. In an interview yesterday at his office, the bishop said that he became "concerned when I learned about the activities of some of the members." Paul referred to what was called a Scotch drinkers' club frequented by Calgary's former Chief of Police Calvin Smoke. The club met once a month at a local restaurant. One of the regular members, Dr. Joseph Jones, has been charged with murder and possession of child pornography.

Wayne Pike, the owner of the restaurant, has been charged with trafficking after the discovery of more than five kilos of cocaine in the trunk of his Mercedes.

Bishop Paul said, "Chief Smoke would often talk about police politics and investigations as the evening wore on. It was upon reflection that I realized that Jones and Pike would pay particular attention at these times."

When asked if he was trying to distance himself from his affiliation with the Scotch drinkers' club and recent allegations, Bishop Paul replied, "God will judge my actions."

Acting Deputy Chief Cameron Harper responded to Bishop Paul's allegations with, "The investigation into the activities of former Police Chief Smoke is ongoing. The allegations are serious, and we are in the process of verifying them."

When asked if the Calgary Police Service has received a black eye because of the activities of the Scotch drinkers' club, Harper said, "Of course we have."

"How's it going with Dr. Alexandre?" Loraine held her son Ben on her knee. They sat in one of the chairs on Lane and Arthur's deck. The boy was already half her height.

"So you and Ben were just in the neighbourhood and dropped in to say hello?" Lane asked, then thought, *Why are you being so suspicious?* Roz got up and hid behind the flowerpot.

"Your emotional response is a sign that things are coming along. In fact, I'd even say that things are going well." Ben stuck his fist in his mouth, then pulled it out. His eyes opened wide after he gagged. Loraine swiped her fingers along her tongue and patted down a rebellious lock of Ben's blond hair. The hair stood back up again after she finished.

"I'm sorry. Let me try again. I see Alexandre again on Monday. We're talking. She's listening. You were right — I have some things to work out." Lane watched Roz poke her head out from behind the flowerpot. *Even Roz heard the combative tone in my voice.*

Loraine smiled.

"It ain't pretty," Lane said. "You know, dealing with this kind of stuff. . . it's messy."

As if to confirm Lane's observation, Ben barfed down the front of his T-shirt.

Lane stood up, went into the kitchen, and returned with about two metres of paper towel.

"It's not that much!" Loraine laughed as she wiped up the mess and took off the baby's T-shirt to reveal Ben's ample belly.

Lane held open a plastic bag. Loraine dropped the T-shirt inside. He rolled up the bag and set it next to what Loraine called Ben's "wardrobe"— a backpack stuffed with all manner of baby essentials.

"Where are Christine and Matt?" Loraine asked.

"At work. They both got jobs at the same golf course.

Today, Christine is driving the beer cart. I'm think she's beginning to like the tips." Lane reached for Ben. The baby leaned away from him and tucked his head next to Loraine's neck.

"He's just started being shy in the last week. So, Christine is driving a *beer cart*?" Loraine raised her eyebrows.

Lane laughed. "First she works in a coffee shop, then she drives a beer cart. That girl's on her way to hell!"

"Oh." Loraine's face took on an air of innocence. "Her mother's been by to denounce her again?"

"No. Apparently that's died down. I guess excommunication is a one-time thing. Which is sort of fortunate when you think about it. Just drive up, do an excommunication, and drive away. Wash your hands of the child." Lane watched Ben checking out his own navel. "Drive into the city, tell your daughter you want nothing more to do with her, then go get some shopping done. Just another day."

"So it was a drive-by?" Loraine rolled her eyes.

"Yes, that's an accurate description." Lane stood up. "I think the coffee's ready."

"While you're up, tell Arthur to get out of bed. It's after ten!"

Lane opened the door. "Speaking of partners, how's Lisa?"

"Back to work. Missing Ben. They've got her working at a desk, developing some new investigative software."

He went inside. Lane poured two coffees—black for Loraine, cream and sugar for himself—and went back outside. "I heard the shower. Arthur will be out shortly."

Loraine took a sip. "You still know how to make a great cup of coffee. How's Christine been doing otherwise?"

Lane hesitated. "Better, I think. She seems happier. There's a boyfriend."

"And?" Ben squirmed and Loraine put her coffee down.

"I didn't handle it well at first." Lane felt his face turning red.

"Sounds like a dad thing." Loraine reached into Ben's wardrobe.

"What's that supposed to mean? People keep saying that."

Loraine lifted Ben so he could stand on her knees while she tried to fit a red T-shirt over his head. "I think it's a protective, instinctual reaction. And before I forget, I came by to invite all of you over for dinner." Ben shook his head through the opening in the T-shirt and sat down.

"I figured it was because you'd heard about Arthur."

Loraine stared at Lane. Ben looked at his mother. "There's something wrong with Arthur?"

"He's got breast cancer. We saw the surgeon yesterday."

Loraine sat open-mouthed. Ben squirmed.

Lane began to cry. *Shit! Where did that come from?*

chapter 12

"It's called in." Keely sat in the passenger's seat of the Chevrolet as they drove west along Crowchild Trail.

"So she said ten?" Lane glimpsed the morning mountains when they crested a hill.

Keely nodded.

Why does the time seem odd? Lane thought.

"I want to see what the daughter and the mother are like together. Sometimes that will tell you more about people. Girls who are thirteen or fourteen can really help you to see their parents and the family situation in an accurate light."

That's for sure.

"After this, you want to go for lunch? My dad invited Dylan and me out. My mom keeps smiling about it. And you'll be able to meet my brother."

"It sounds more like a family get-together." Lane saw a car approaching. It was travelling at least twice the speed limit.

"When I told my father we had some work to do, he told me to bring you." Keely spotted the car. "Man, he's in a rush."

They got a glimpse of the driver and recognized the vehicle as an unmarked police cruiser. "Wonder where he's headed?" Keely looked over her shoulder to see if the car was turning north or south.

"Anything to add to the plan for how we're going to handle Jelena and Zacki?" Lane asked.

Keely took a moment to think. "I'd like to ask more questions about the Branimir and Goran connection. Then if you could ask one of those oddball questions like you did the other night. You know, the ones that get people off-balance, so they end up saying more than they planned."

Lane nodded as he took his foot off the accelerator and flipped the right-turn indicator. The northern hillside on Calgary's edge was a maze of condominiums. The road led to a golf course. He turned right and up the hill. On their left, acreages skirted the perimeter of the members–only golf course. They passed a supermarket and a gas station. On their right lay a green space.

"These new communities have only one access road," Keely said. "Makes it kind of difficult."

Lane spotted a red plastic container tucked up against the curb. It looked like it might hold eight litres. The top was duct-taped closed. And the container was taped to the concrete.

It's all wrong, he thought as they drove closer.

His foot jammed down against the accelerator. The Chevy's engine hesitated, then roared. He changed into the left-hand lane.

"Get down!"

Keely looked at Lane. He saw her silhouetted by light.

The concussion hit the rear of the Chevy, lifting the right rear wheel off the pavement. The rear window bowed in and turned opaque. Lane felt a blow to his chest cavity. It pounded the air from his lungs. The Chevy rolled up onto its front left tire and then onto its roof. It thumped over the grass median, jumped the curb, and screamed over pavement. The grill hit the guardrail on the far side of the roadway. The airbags exploded in Lane's and Keely's faces.

Lane felt detached from the experience as he listened to debris raining down onto the underside of the Chevy. *The heavy-duty thunks must be bits of concrete or pavement. We're kind of lucky the car is upside-down.* He looked to his left at a guardrail about twenty centimetres from his nose. He put his hands over his head in an attempt to ease the pressure of the seat belt on his abdomen. Then he looked to his right. A droplet of blood spattered the fabric on the Chev's roof liner. Another followed.

"Keely?" He tried to see if her eyes were open.

"Don't yell. I've got a headache." Keely put her hands on the roof.

"Are you okay?"

"Man, are you in trouble. My dad is going to be so mad at you. We'll miss lunch because of this." She turned to him and smiled as blood rolled through her hair and dripped onto the roof liner, forming a pattern of red dots.

$$\times$$

"Stop moving! She's okay. It looks like a scalp wound. A few stitches and she'll be fine. All she has is a headache. She's being taken to emergency as a precaution. So far, it doesn't look like she has a concussion." The paramedic checked Lane's eyes and peripheral vision. "How do your chest and abdomen feel?"

The siren of Keely's ambulance wailed as it drove away. Lane watched an officer move his cruiser to allow the ambulance to pass.

Lane looked north and south. Cruisers with their flashing blue and red lights blocked all four lanes. The muscles in his neck ached.

A fire engine was parked near the upside-down wreck of the Chevy. Two firemen with shovels were spreading something that looked like kitty litter on the ground to soak up spilled fuel. The bomb squad and Forensics Unit were taking measurements and marking bits of debris. *Must be looking for what's left of the bomb.*

One of the investigators looked Lane's way and began to walk over. He was wearing a face shield and white bunny suit. *What does Fibre want?*

"How are you feeling, Detective Lane?" Fibre removed his face shield and pulled his hood back.

Lane moved his shoulders. "Sore all over."

"I wanted to talk with you before they take you to the hospital. Did you see anything before the explosion?" Fibre removed his eye shield and cradled it over his abdomen.

"There was a red plastic container duct-taped to the curb." Lane closed his eyes, trying to remember.

"Volume?" Fibre asked.

"Five to ten litres." Lane opened his eyes. "Best guess."

"Anything else?"

"I tried to get out of the way, but wasn't fast enough."

"More evidence of your intuition. You reacted before the explosion. It probably saved Ms. Saliba's life. The concussion would have hit her side of the vehicle first. Your clear recollections suggest you haven't suffered a concussion. Very good news. Now you can go to the hospital." Fibre looked at the EMT. "The detective is ready." Fibre looked at Lane. "There is a preliminary finding that is unusual. There is no evidence of metallic projectiles perforating your vehicle or scattered around the site. Improvised explosive devices are notorious for containing all sorts of shrapnel. An anomaly for you to think about." Fibre pulled his hood on, turned, and adjusted his face shield as he walked away.

"Let's get you to the hospital," said the EMT.

"We have to make a stop first," Lane replied.

The driver looked over his shoulder. "No stops. We're going to the hospital."

Lane stepped away from the ambulance. He smiled. "You both need a coffee, and I need to tell my partner's family that she's all right. It needs to be done face to face."

The driver and EMT looked at one another.

"What's it going to be?" Lane asked.

A voice came from behind the southern police barrier.

"I'm late for my tee time!" Lane and the EMTs looked in the direction of the disturbance. A man in white shorts stood on the far side of the yellow tape. He looked at his watch. "I can't be late! Let me through."

The officer on this side of the tape crossed his arms. "Cuff him and put him in the back of the cruiser!" the EMT said.

The man in white looked at the ambulance, then at the officer, got into his Cadillac, and promptly backed into the vehicle behind him.

"From bad to worse," a fireman said.

Ten minutes later, the ambulance stopped outside the front door of a family restaurant just north of Crowchild Trail. Lane stepped down from the rear of the ambulance. "I'll be right back," he said.

"If you fall, there'll be hell to pay," the EMT said.

Lane smiled, entered the restaurant, and sidled past the line of people waiting for a seat. He found Amir, Katherine, and Dylan drinking coffee. Amir looked at his watch, then toward the door. He turned white when he recognized Lane.

Katherine looked at her husband, followed his line of sight, and paled as well. Dylan glanced past Lane to see where Keely was.

"She's okay," Lane said. "I saw her and she's okay. Just needs a few stitches. She's been taken to the Foothills Medical Centre as a precaution."

"You look like hell," Katherine said.

Amir slid over. "We have to go!"

"And Dylan is going to drive." Lane stood next to Amir, blocking him from getting out of his seat. "Okay?" Lane put his hand, still bloody from holding it against the cut on Keely's scalp, on Amir's shoulder.

"My daughter's blood?" asked Katherine.

Lane nodded.

Amir turned to Dylan. He reached into his pocket and handed the keys over.

"Just follow the ambulance. That way we'll all get there at the same time." Lane turned. They followed him outside.

✕

"You must love this place."

Lane recognized the voice as he sat in the vinyl chair next to a bed in the emergency room. Harper stepped through the gap between the curtains. He was wearing his deputy police chief's uniform. He shook Lane's hand. "Detective Saliba okay?"

Lane nodded. "As far as I know, her only injury is a scalp wound."

Harper sat on the edge of the bed. "How about you? It looks like someone dragged you behind a horse."

"My muscles are starting to seize up. Just bruises and sprains. How are you doing?"

Harper leaned closer. "Looking under rocks and finding all sorts of crap that Smoke and his gang hid. Man, it's a mess. He's made the entire force look like a joke."

Lane closed his eyes. "Or he's made himself into a joke."

"You okay?"

"Just tired. Arthur's on his way. He'll pick me up, drive me home, and let the kids interrogate me." Lane smiled. "It's good to see you."

"Chief Simpson sent me down to check on you and Saliba. You know it has to be this way until the investigation is over?" Harper glanced at the floor.

"I understand, believe me."

"The bomb was meant for you and Saliba?"

"Yes. Definitely." Lane's mind moved into crisp, sharp focus.

"Any idea who?" Harper asked.

"Yes. There are two possibilities. Either it's connected to the disappearance of Andelko Branimir, or it's related to the threats against Keely. And I'm convinced that threat comes from inside the department."

"A cop?"

"Almost certainly. The letters, the pipe bomb, and the lack of physical evidence all point in that direction."

"How's Arthur doing? Erinn and I heard about the cancer."

Lane shrugged. "Lori told you?"

Harper nodded.

"Surgery is on Friday."

chapter 13

Lane sat across from Dr. Alexandre. Both sipped their coffees.

"Isn't a psychiatrist supposed to serve soothing tea?" Lane asked.

"You're getting your sense of humour back." Alexandre set her coffee down and smoothed her skirt. "To answer your question, I enjoy coffee. So do you."

"You continue to do your homework, then?"

"Of course. I don't like to go into a session knowing nothing about the patient. And this patient. . ." Alexandre closed her eyes and touched her forehead for effect. ". . .was recently involved in an accident." She looked at the ceiling as if asking for guidance from a supreme being, "In fact, I would hazard a guess that you've been too close to the light in your recent past."

"Very impressive. What tipped you off?"

Alexandre smiled for the first time. "I listen to the news, and you have the beginnings of some bruising on the side of your face. Also, you're moving carefully, like your entire body is hurting."

Lane nodded.

"How is your partner?" Alexandre asked. "I mean your detective partner."

"She got eight stitches for a scalp wound. I'll go and visit her after this." Lane frowned.

"Do you know who set off the device?" Alexandre asked.

"Not yet." Lane heard his voice change.

"So you're on the hunt?"

"I guess so." *So that's what this is called. It is as primal as that. I'm a hunter.*

"Last visit, we talked about you being punished for saving your brother."

Lane took a long breath. "Just like my last major case, which involved two sisters. The stepfather abused the older sister, named Maddy. Her younger sibling was about to be abused. We got the father. The sisters are okay. Or at least, they're healing. My reward was being put under investigation for the loss of a firearm."

"Anything else?"

"When my father was dying, he forgot about the recent past and only remembered me as a child. He accepted me all over again, and then he died. Now my brother and his wife want to sweep me back into the closet, get me to sign away any claim to my childhood, and disappear. I risked my life at the river to save my brother Joseph. When I think back on it, I was the one in the family who was drowning. It started to bother me again after Maddy's stepfather tried to pull out his gun. It triggered memories of the day my brother almost drowned. There's a moment when you either act or you don't. I saved Joseph's life. I saved a child and her older sister. I couldn't figure out why I was suddenly persona non grata. Before those two experiences, I never understood the statement, 'No good deed goes unpunished.' Being punished for doing my job. Being punished for saving Joseph's life. Being excommunicated from my family. Seeing my father after so many years. Having my own family. Having to do the work I do." Lane stopped. *Why am I running off at the mouth like this?*

"Okay then. Are you tired of feeling sorry for yourself?"

And you call yourself a doctor?! Lane opened his mouth, but closed it when he saw the doctor smiling for a second time.

"Sometimes depression can be the absence of emotion. It's like eating bland food. It tastes neither wonderful nor terrible. It simply tastes like nothing."

Lane snorted. "Then anger is a sign of healing?"

"In this case, I'd say so." The doctor reached for her coffee.

Lane saw her Adam's apple. "What's it like?"

The doctor sat back in her chair and held the coffee with both hands in front of her, as if to fend off Lane's question. "What's what like?"

"You know, juggling past, present, job, and family?"

Alexandre thought for a moment. "That's the trick, isn't it? Learning how to juggle it all." She set the coffee down. "Speaking of juggling, how are things on the home front?"

"Arthur has breast cancer. It looks like the surgery will be at the end of the week."

She studied him. "You really are juggling right now. What's the prognosis?"

"We don't know yet."

"We need to start thinking about having the whole family in for a session when Arthur is back on his feet."

×

Lane knocked on the door of the two-storey, sand-coloured condo where Keely and her family were staying. In his other hand was a tray with three cups of coffee.

"Who's there?"

"It's me, Lane."

The door opened wide enough for Amir to see him. "Come in." Amir looked past Lane and shut the door.

"How's Keely feeling?" Lane asked.

Amir pointed down the hall. "In the kitchen."

Lane walked down the hall and set the coffees on the table. He looked sideways at Keely, who sat near the window. The right side of her face was beginning to bruise. Another bruise and a series of stitches were visible along her scalp line.

"Thanks for the coffee," Keely said.

Lane handed one cup to her and one to Amir, who sat down beside his daughter. Lane took a sip from his cup and watched her. "Where does it hurt?" He smiled and winced.

She smiled back and grimaced. "You know as well as I do that it hurts everywhere."

"I'm going to talk with Fibre. You want to come?" Lane asked.

Amir said, "Kharra alhek."

Keely held up her hand, "Let me finish my coffee, then I'll get ready. Dad, it's rude to say 'Shit on you' to Lane."

Amir didn't appear the least bit embarrassed. "The doctor says she needs to rest!"

"It's okay, dad — we're just going to talk with a guy who can give us some answers. There's no danger involved." Keely set her coffee down. "I'm gonna get dressed."

Amir said, "Majnoon."

"Dad. Look at me. This is my decision, not his." Keely hugged her father. "By the way, Lane's not crazy, and I'll be careful." She made her way to her bedroom and closed the door.

"What happened to your last partner? Did he get killed?" Amir asked.

Lane kept his tone matter-of-fact and didn't smile, even though he wanted to. "He's the acting deputy police chief."

Amir went to reply and stopped. He looked thoughtfully at Lane. They drank their coffees in silence for ten minutes.

Keely opened her bedroom door and went to the bathroom.

Amir finished his coffee. "Keely said you stayed with her in the car until the fire department got you out."

"She was bleeding and my door was up against a guardrail. I didn't want to move her in case there were other injuries." *Stick to the facts,* Lane thought.

"She said you just talked to her."

"That's right. I was worried she might have a concussion."

Amir looked at his coffee. "You could have left her there and got out."

Lane shook his head. "No, I couldn't."

Amir studied Lane but said nothing. They heard Keely's footsteps and turned as she approached. Amir got up and went to hug her. She winced in pain as he put her arms around her shoulders. "We won't be long," she said.

×

Lane parked the Jeep in front of the glass-and-metal office building that was part of the Foothills Medical Centre where Fibre worked.

"I'm sorry about my father," Keely said.

Lane smiled. "Don't take this the wrong way, but I like the guy."

Keely laughed and grimaced. "Oooh, that hurts. Even when he's swearing at you in Arabic?"

"Especially when he's swearing at me in Arabic. It's what Arthur does. And what your dad doesn't know is that I understood all of what he said."

Keely laughed and moaned.

"You hungry?" Lane asked.

"Starved."

Lane reached for his cell, flipped it open, and dialed. He looked at Keely.

"Yes, Dr. Weaver?" Lane listened, then said, "We'd like to meet for lunch. Yes, perhaps a bit unusual. Yes, I'm sure you always bring your lunch. Yes, today is different. We'd like you to come with us and get a little fresh air. Yes, both of us are in the car outside waiting for you. We'll wait for a minute until you get here." Lane closed the phone.

"Do you think he'll come out?" Keely asked

"We'll give him five minutes. Apparently, he enjoys routine." Lane looked sideways at her and raised his eyebrows.

Keely leaned against the door. "How did you know about the bomb?"

"What do you mean?"

"Just before the explosion, you changed lanes and I can remember the roar of the engine." She looked out the window, seeing it happen again.

"Flashback?" Lane asked.

"Yes. A flashback. Answer the question." Keely turned to look at him.

"Something wasn't right. I saw the plastic container duct-taped to the curb and the pavement. And it looked like the top was taped closed. It was an instinctive reaction to something that was out of place."

"So it would have exploded much closer to me if you hadn't reacted the way you did."

Lane nodded.

"Thank you. I owe you."

"Let's get one thing clear," Lane said. "You don't owe me a thing. We're partners."

"Grumpy?" Keely smiled.

"A little."

"Would you look at that?" Keely pointed.

Fibre stood outside. He looked from side to side. Lane started the engine and pulled around to pick the doctor up. Fibre had trouble opening the back door but finally managed to get in the back seat. He searched for the seat belt.

"Thank you for joining us, Colin," Lane said. "Please close the door."

"Oh, yes, of course." Fibre closed the door. "Ready."

Lane looked at Fibre in the mirror. The doctor sat with his lunch bag on his lap.

Ten minutes later, they parked near the river and close to a crescent where a wicker furniture store, a fabric shop, and a couple of apartments faced a restaurant in a permanent state of expansion and renovation.

Lane groaned as he exited the car. Keely did the same.

Fibre got out, closed his door, and went inside the restaurant without a backwards glance. Lane followed and held the door open for Keely.

Inside, they found an almost exclusively female clientele casting sideways glances at Fibre's glamour-boy face and physique.

Lane looked at Keely to see if she'd noticed. She smiled back, shook her head, and mouthed a single word: "Unbelievable."

They sat down across from the doctor, who was studying the menu, which was written in a variety of colours on a whiteboard on the wall behind the cash register. "Thought I'd better get a table. Are the Nanaimo bars good here?"

"Delicious. You've had them before," Lane said.

"I'll have two." Fibre opened his lunch bag, unwrapped a sandwich, and began to eat while looking out the window. Lane caught a whiff of peanut butter and jam that smelled of saskatoon berries.

Lane and Keely decided on what to have for lunch and got up to order.

"My treat," Keely said.

"No," Lane said.

"Yes." She glared at Lane. He put his money back in his pocket. "It's the least I can do. You saved my life and my father insulted you for it. At least as far as you and I go, one good turn should be rewarded."

After they sat down and the coffee had arrived, Fibre looked at them. "Initial findings are that the rear of your vehicle took the brunt of the explosive force and absorbed most of its energy. The explosive device was a mixture of nitro methane and ammonium nitrate. We believe that a cellphone was used to trigger the device. No nails, ball bearings, or other bits of metal were found nearby. Devices like this often use shrapnel. This one did not." Fibre looked side to side as he rolled up the sandwich wrapper, folded up the bag, and tucked the wrap inside a fold. He opened his jacket pocket and slid the bag inside.

The waiter brought sandwiches on thick slices of kettle bread to Lane and Keely. Fibre stared at the plate with its pair of Nanaimo bars; to him it appeared to be the only food in the café. Lane sipped his coffee and watched Fibre slice off one corner with his fork, speared it, and put the morsel in his mouth. His eyes went wide, then closed as he swallowed and smiled. *He looks like he's about to have an orgasm!* Fibre's eyes opened. He cut off another section of Nanaimo bar, repeating the process all over again.

After the fourth bite, Lane looked around. Some of the women stared, a few looked away, and one dabbed her forehead with a napkin.

"Anything new on the pipe bomb?" Keely asked.

Fibre opened his eyes and reoriented himself within his surroundings. "No. The device is clean. We checked for blood, skin cells, and fingerprints. The bombmaker was very cautious about leaving evidence behind."

Lane began to eat his sandwich. He watched Keely cut off small bites of bread with a knife. She saw him watching her. "My jaw hurts."

"I'm finished." Fibre stood up and went outside. He stood waiting by the car until Lane and Keely arrived five minutes later. They traveled in silence back to Fibre's office. He closed the back door of the Chev and walked into the building, all without a wave, a thank-you, a backward glance, or a goodbye.

"Very odd," Keely said.

"And very good at his job. He grows on you after a couple of years." *I never thought I would say that.*

"So what's next?" Keely asked.

"Wait for a break?" Lane didn't have to wait long for Keely's reaction.

"No way. We're getting close. Either it's someone inside the force or it's Jelena."

"You sound like it's getting personal," Lane said.

She looked at him. "Somebody tried to kill us. You bet it's personal. Who do we concentrate on?"

"The bomber is the most immediate threat." Lane rubbed what was left of his earlobe.

"You think it's the same one who blew up my car?" Keely asked.

"I think it was someone who knew we'd be at a certain place at a certain time." Lane looked at Keely.

"I looked at the map again. The route we took is actually one of two roads into that development. There is another way in, but it would take a lot longer, and it's more complicated." Keely leaned away from the door and rubbed her right shoulder.

"So the most likely suspects would be Jelena or whoever had access to our communications. When did you call it in?"

Keely thought for a moment. "About thirty minutes before we left my place. That gave the bomber at least forty-five minutes to get everything in place."

"Plenty of time. We should expect that there are more explosive devices available to the bomber."

"That's a given. Then we need to ask ourselves if Mladen would have access to the information." Keely massaged her temples.

"Not likely."

"Is the bomber after me or both of us?" Keely asked.

"We'll know that only after the bomber is caught."

"Take me home. I need some rest. We'll get back at it tomorrow." Keely closed her eyes.

Lane started the engine.

×

"Yesterday you almost get blown up, and today you go back to work! Are you nuts?" Christine stood over Lane. He was sitting on the couch with his feet up.

Lane looked at Matt and Arthur for support. Daniel looked at the front door as if searching for an escape route.

Matt said, "She's right."

Arthur put his fists on his hips. "You'll get no sympathy from me!"

Lane looked at Daniel. A glare from Christine froze her boyfriend in place.

"Are you ready?" Matt asked.

"For what?" Lane asked.

Roz tilted her head to one side and gave him a quizzical look.

"For dinner at Lisa and Loraine's." Christine rolled her eyes.

"Why didn't you remind me?" Lane asked.

"We did," Matt said.

Lane drove while Arthur, Matt, Christine, and Daniel talked.

It took twenty-five minutes to drive to Lisa and Loraine's house, which was situated on a street lined with mature trees, a motor home or two, and several aged automobiles. There were cars parked on either side of the street in front of their house. "Somebody's having a party," Lane said.

"Ya think?" Christine asked.

The inside of the car was quiet as he parked half a block away. They climbed out of the Jeep. Arthur took two bottles of wine and a gift for the baby from the back of the vehicle.

Lane followed the four as they walked up the sidewalk to the front door. A note was taped to the glass: GO AROUND BACK.

When they reached the side of the house, they heard voices

and laughter. A baby said something delightfully unintelligible. Another tiny voice said, "Mom? Mom!"

They rounded the corner. Lane saw familiar faces.

Harper's daughter Jessica climbed up into his arms. Harper walked toward Lane and offered his hand. "A clandestine meeting. Everyone here can keep this meeting secret, I hope." He rolled his eyes.

"Good to see you." Lane smiled and received a hug from Erinn, Harper's redheaded wife.

She said, "We've missed you."

Jessica wrapped her arms around her father's neck and glared at Lane.

"She remembers me!" Lane said.

Erinn laughed. "She's daddy's girl and thinks you've come to take him away from her."

Arthur was getting a group hug from Lisa and Loraine and their infant son Ben. Christine and Matt introduced Daniel to Harper's nephew Glenn.

Lane looked over Erinn's shoulder. Keely stood behind Loraine. Lisa released Arthur and turned, Ben squirming in her arms, wanting to be put down on the grass.

He heard Keely say, "My dad told Dylan he was going to have to convert if he wants to marry me."

"What does your mom think of that?" Loraine asked.

"She wouldn't convert when they got married. She thinks going to Catholic school for eleven years was more than anyone should be asked to do in the religious department." Keely kicked her sandals off.

"Eleven years?" Loraine asked.

"She got kicked out of school at the end of Grade Eleven. There was a discussion about the rights of women as they're written in the Bible. She stood up and said there are no rights for women as far as the Bible or the Catholic Church are concerned. She got suspended for being disrespectful and confrontational. She finished up her Grade Twelve in another school. Then she went into law."

Dylan walked out the screen door with a beer in one hand and a soft drink in the other. He handed the soft drink to Keely, took a swig of the beer, and asked, "Do you want me to convert?"

"Eavesdropping again?" Keely asked. "Do you want to?"

Dylan blushed and shook his head. "No."

"Then don't." Keely looked at Lane. "Are you surprised?"

Christine laughed. "The legendary deductive skills of Detective Lane! He had no idea that all of you would be here."

Harper laughed. "Since we're talking about your reputation — you've wrecked three cars in the last year or so. Could you give me a rough estimate on how many you'll need for next year? We're in the middle of budget negotiations."

Lisa hugged Lane, and baby Ben squirmed between them. "I hear you're getting on-the-job training with high explosives."

Lane winced. "Just trying to stay current on the latest data concerning injuries caused by improvised explosive devices."

Keely laughed. "Yes, Detective Lane believes in hands-on training methods. Since explosive devises are becoming more and more common, he decided to make them part of our investigation and part of my training regimen. So far, I've had first-hand experience with two types of explosions."

Harper raised a bottle of beer. "Careful, Keely — it gets even more interesting from here on in!"

Erinn said, "I'm just glad you're both in one piece."

"Can we talk about something else?" Christine reached for Ben. Lisa handed him off. Then Daniel reached for Ben. Ben smiled, turned to Christine, and grabbed the collar of her sleeveless top. "Hey, Ben! Watch what you're grabbing!" she said.

Arthur touched Lane on the shoulder. "What can I get you?" he asked.

"A cold beer, please." Lane sat down and was joined by Keely, Loraine, Erinn, Lisa, Arthur, and Harper. Soon, Dylan, Christine, Glenn, and Matt were playing with the younger children. The older people sat in a circle of lawn chairs.

Lane listened to the conversations swirling around him. *Mladen lost all of this. What would I do if someone took my family away?*

Erinn asked, "When do you go in for your surgery, Arthur?"

The party fell quiet.

Arthur looked over her head. "It's not one hundred percent for sure yet. I have an appointment tomorrow. But it looks like Friday."

"That's quick," Lisa said.

"Anything we can do to help?" Harper asked.

"Now that you mention it, you can keep Lane from being blown up or shot," Arthur said.

Harper raised his glass and said, "To long life and good friends."

chapter 14

"Detective Lane?"

Lane recognized the voice. He tucked the phone next to his ear and held it there with his shoulder while he sat on the edge of the bed. He glanced at the clock; it was just after five in the morning. "Chief Simpson."

"I just got off the phone with the defense lawyer for Officer Stockwell. Stockwell is to be charged with the bombing of Officer Saliba's vehicle. Is it possible for you to view the interrogation as a bystander? Is Detective Saliba well enough to be there also?"

"I think so. She'll be my next call." Lane stood up. His ribs ached from the bruises left by the seat belt and the airbags.

"How was Stockwell's involvement uncovered?" Lane asked.

"I'll leave that up to the discretion of the investigator in charge to decide how much information to share with you."

"I see." *I wonder who the source is?*

"How long will you be?" Simpson asked.

Lane looked at the clock. "Thirty minutes."

"Good." Simpson gave him the name of the investigator and hung up.

Lane dialed. "Keely? There's a suspect in the bombing of your car. Can you make it for the interrogation?"

"Fuckin' right!" she said.

"I'll pick you up in fifteen minutes."

When he drove up to the front door of the condo, Keely was waiting on the curb. As she eased into the Jeep, she said, "Have we got time for a coffee?"

Lane pulled away and said, "Not yet."

"Who is this guy?" Keely snapped her seat belt on.

"He worked in Chief Smoke's office. A member of the Scotch drinkers' club. You'll probably know him to see him. After Smoke left, this guy was put back on the street." Lane accelerated.

"How are you feeling today?" Keely asked.

"Just about every bone and muscle is complaining. I hope I don't sneeze — my ribs are pretty sore." Lane pulled the seat belt away from his chest as he followed the river into the downtown core. "How about you?"

"The headache is gone, and I can move a bit easier. The stitches are healing, so I could wash my hair. It felt great to get rid of all of that grit and dust from the explosion."

"How are your dad and Dylan doing?" Lane drove under a bridge and accelerated along an open stretch of road.

"Mom told Dad to lay off of Dylan. When you phoned, Dylan had already left to go to the university. Things are pretty tense. Dad is still pressuring Dylan to convert." Keely looked out the window at cyclists and joggers using the paved trails between the road and the river.

They drove into downtown and parked inside the wire behind the department building. Keely got out of the Jeep first. She opened the back door to the building and led the way to the elevators. Simpson's secretary waved them through when they arrived at the chief's office.

Lane closed the door behind them. He and Keely eased themselves into chairs. Simpson sat in a third chair to complete the triangle.

"Are you on the mend?" Simpson asked Keely.

Keely nodded. "Better today."

"And you?" Simpson looked at Lane.

"Okay." Lane looked at the paintings of coyotes and bears hanging on the walls.

"Officer Stockwell was apprehended this morning," Simpson said. "He's waiting in an interrogation room. He has been made aware that he is to be charged and has demanded a lawyer and a representative from the union. These individuals are en route. I would like the two of you to observe only. A room has been made available for you to watch the interview."

"Okay," said Lane. He looked at Keely. She nodded.

Simpson went to say something, stopped, thought for a moment, and said, "Very well. When the lawyer and union representative arrive, the interrogation will begin. Dr. Weaver is in an adjacent room. He'll fill you in on some of the evidence." The chief waited.

"Could we get a cup of coffee?" Lane asked.

Simpson smiled. "We'll hook you up." He stood, opened the door, and addressed his secretary. "Can you give these detectives directions to a good cup of coffee?"

The chief shook their hands as they left.

Five minutes later, they arrived at the interrogation rooms. Fibre was waiting for them. He waved them into a room with two chairs and a table. There was a flat-screen television mounted in a corner near the ceiling, and the walls were painted a nondescript colour. "This is what we have so far."

Lane looked at a small cardboard box containing the mangled end cap of the pipe bomb and three typed letters in separate envelopes.

Fibre pointed at the end cap. "We have receipts connecting Stockwell to the purchase of pipe and end caps consistent with the remains of the pipe bomb. Also, the paper and printer used for the threatening letters addressed to Detective Saliba are a match to the printer Stockwell has access to and has been observed using."

Lane stared at the evidence on the table. *I wonder who will do the interview and if he has any other evidence. Everything here is purely circumstantial.*

Fibre put the evidence into the cardboard box, picked it up, and left the room.

Keely and Lane sat down and looked up at the TV. They saw an officer wearing a white shirt and blue tie sitting at a table with a file folder in front of him. His hair was cut short and he had the face of a choirboy.

"You know him?" Keely asked.

"Yes." Lane watched the man on camera. "It's John Buck. He investigates complaints about police officers. I don't know him well. In a minute or two, we'll see how good he is and what he's got."

Stockwell entered the room and walked around to the far side of the table. He was wearing black boots and jodhpurs: the uniform of a motorcycle cop. Lane noticed his close-cropped military haircut, the immaculate creases on his blue shirt, and the way his tie was tucked between two shirt buttons.

"That's Stockwell?" Keely asked.

"Yep."

"He was a regular at the Scotch drinkers' club," Keely said.

The door opened. A man in a grey suit entered and shook hands with Stockwell. "His name is Al Roper. He was in the club too." Keely shook her head and looked disgusted.

"Al Roper is one of the top defense lawyers in the city," Lane said.

Five minutes later, the union rep arrived. He was six foot four and had a barrel chest and clean-shaven head.

Keely sighed. "That's Art Lesley. Another member of the club." She looked at Lane.

Either she's feeling it's hopeless or she's angry about having to see the good ol' boys again. "We'll see if Buck can use it to his advantage."

"How?" Keely asked.

Buck is alone in a room full of testosterone. "He knows more than they do. That's his advantage."

They watched Roper sit on one side of Stockwell and Lesley sit on the other. Buck stood up and reached across the table to shake hands with each of the men facing him. "This conversation is being recorded." *His voice is very soft, almost apologetic.*

"Of course," Roper said. Lane heard the arrogance in the man's voice.

"We have several pieces of evidence to bring forward," said Buck. "Officer Stockwell, this is your opportunity to reveal your deliberate intimidation of Detective Saliba, a fellow officer on loan to the police service."

Stockwell looked at the file in front of Buck.

"I've advised my client not to answer any questions with regard to Detective Saliba," Roper said.

"As you will." Buck pulled out one of the letters and began to read. "'Rats get exterminated in this department.' This letter was written by you, mailed by you, and received by Detective Saliba." Buck looked at Stockwell, who began to open his mouth. "No, don't speak. You had your chance."

"This partial print was found on the envelope. It's a match with your fingerprint." Buck opened the file and put a photocopy on the table.

"Don't know how that got there." Stockwell wiped sweat from his forehead.

"No, don't say anything. Officer Stockwell. It is your right to refrain from answering questions. Please, follow your lawyer's advice." Lesley put his hand on Stockwell's shoulder.

Roper yawned. "As Officer Stockwell said, he doesn't know how the fingerprint got there — if in fact it *is* his fingerprint."

"Another odd fact," Buck continued, "is the paper and the printer used to produce the letters. All have been traced to a printer in this building that Officer Stockwell has access to and makes frequent use of." Buck pulled out another letter and read, "'The thing about rats is that they breed quickly, so extermination must be swift and violent.'"

"Great!" Roper said. "Let's take this evidence to court as soon as possible!" He smiled at his client. "The evidence is so circumstantial that I can't wait to discredit it — and you, Staff Sergeant Buck!" Roper shook his head and smiled at his joke.

Buck pulled out the evidence bag and the end cap from a pipe bomb. He held up the label on the evidence bag. "We have receipts in the name of the accused. He purchased this pipe and these end caps."

"So he did some work around the house." Roper looked at Lesley. "He brought us down here for this?"

Buck loosened his tie. He opened the folder.

Roper smiled. "Getting too hot in here for you, officer?"

Buck kept his voice low. "We have a witness," he said, "who will testify that you said, 'I taped the bomb to her fuel tank. It was easy. And the pipe bomb worked like a charm.'"

Roper and Lesley leaned forward.

"As a result of the witness statement, we followed the procedures for tapping and taping." Buck passed copies of documents to Lesley and Roper. "You can read along with your lawyer if you like, Mr. Stockwell."

Lane glanced away from the screen to see Keely's reaction. "Now this is getting interesting," she said.

Buck pulled more documents from his file. "We have transcripts of taped conversations between Mr. Stockwell and another member of the police service. I have one part of a conversation highlighted for you." Buck slid copies to Lesley and Roper.

Roper read the page and looked sideways at Stockwell as he passed the page to his client.

"According to the transcript you said, 'After what Saliba did to Smoke, she needed to be taught a lesson. The bitch is a rat. I'm glad the second explosion put her in the hospital. Maybe her and her fag partner will find another line of work now,' Copies of the taped conversations in their entirety will be made available to the three of you."

Buck closed his folder and stood. "I need to inform you, Mr. Stockwell, that the next step is to have you removed as a member of the Calgary Police Service. Also, the crown prosecutor has been made aware of the charges against you. You are to appear in court in two days' time. When you leave this room, you will be processed and have the specific charges explained to you."

"I had nothing to do with the second bomb!" Stockwell crossed his arms.

"Shut up!" Roper said.

Buck stood, picked up his folder, and left the room. A minute later, Lane heard a knock on the door. Keely opened it. "May I come in?" Buck asked.

Lane saw that the knot of Buck's tie was once again tucked neatly at the top of his collar.

Buck shut the door.

"Loosening the tie was part of the performance." Lane said.

"Mr. Roper was hoping to make me sweat, and I didn't want to disappoint." Buck stood with his back to the door.

"Very nice work," Keely said.

Buck smiled. "I've debated whether to speak with you. I wanted you both to hear and see the evidence we have against Mr. Stockwell. There is more information, however."

Lane looked at Keely.

"Like what?" Keely asked.

"There are a series of conversations on the transcripts." Buck set his file on the table, leaned back against the door, and crossed his arms. "Two names — a pair of detectives — are mentioned quite often. A former police chief offered a two-hundred-dollar bottle of Scotch to anyone who could discredit or intimidate either of the detectives. Am I being clear enough with my generalizations?"

"I think so," Keely said.

"Apparently the former police chief was upset for two reasons. First, a female officer uncovered some disconcerting facts about a club the chief belonged to, and he was embarrassed as a result. Second, the chief felt his reputation was tarnished by a male officer who discovered the illegal activities of a close associate." Buck looked at the floor for a moment. "It's important to understand that the former chief put great value in his reputation and his position."

Lane said, "Isn't that kind of ironic?"

"Not if you understand that we're talking about a sociopath. Then it almost makes sense, and it makes Stockwell's actions predictable considering the social environment." Buck watched Lane and Keely and waited for a reaction.

"I wondered sometimes if there were only a few of us who saw, really saw, what was going on," Lane said.

"Don't you think it's a bit presumptuous to assume that only a few police officers could be intelligent enough to see that a very unhealthy climate was created by the network of male officers who advanced each other's careers based on their membership in a misogynistic drinking club?" Buck looked at Lane and Keely in turn.

"Are you assuming there weren't a few women who saw what was going on?" Keely asked.

"Point taken. Please understand that I am just explaining this to you, and I am asking you not to discuss this matter with anyone else." Buck moved away from the door.

"We hear you," Keely said.

"Thank you," Lane said.

Buck picked up his file and left.

×

Arthur was waiting for Lane when he came through the front door. "Daniel is here. Behave yourself."

Lane smiled. "It's great to be home."

"You seem pleased with yourself." Arthur led the way into the kitchen.

"Well?" Lane asked.

"Well what?" Arthur asked.

"What's new on the hospital front?"

"I have a series of medical tests starting tomorrow. And the operation is on for Friday. I can't eat after lunch on Thursday, and I need to be at the Foothills at eight o'clock in the morning." Arthur tried to smile. "So, come on. Tell me what happened."

"You remember Stockwell?" Lane breathed in the scent of salmon baking in maple syrup and ginger.

"Hard to forget someone like that. Is this a time for celebration?"

Lane reached into the fridge and pulled out a beer. "You want one?"

Arthur nodded. "You sure this isn't a wine celebration?"

Lane looked at the beer. "No, this is definitely a cold beer celebration." He reached into the fridge for a second beer, fetched two tall glasses, and poured. "Cheers."

There was the sound of feet taking the stairs two at a time. Daniel landed on the kitchen floor and took in the beer, Arthur, and Lane. His smile flatlined. "Just came up to get a drink."

"Would you like a beer?" Lane asked.

Arthur smiled.

"Sure." Daniel tried on his best smile.

Lane got up, pulled a beer out of the fridge, and poured. "Cheers." He handed the beer to Daniel.

Daniel hesitated, took the glass, and sipped tentatively. "Good stuff. What's the occasion?"

"Things are coming together. I can feel it." Lane smiled at Arthur.

Daniel went downstairs. "You'll never guess what just happened," he said to Christine, trying to keep his voice low.

"What?"

"Nice work." Arthur smiled. "And what about Stockwell?"

"He's being charged with the first bomb." Lane took a sip of beer and sighed.

"What about the second bomb?"

Lane closed his eyes, savouring the beer. "He says he had nothing to do with that."

"Do you believe him?" Arthur asked.

"I don't know." Lane thought for a moment. "I really don't know."

"How did Keely handle it?"

Lane smiled. "Like a pro."

"Did you tell *her* that?"

chapter 15

"Take another bow for your work." Lane lifted his coffee in a salute to Keely. They sat at Central Blends, where the coffee was smooth, the food was cooked fresh on the premises, and the atmosphere was rustic.

Keely smiled. "The best part is that since Stockwell's been charged, we moved back home yesterday. Dylan couldn't have handled much more of living with my dad."

Lane nodded, then sipped his coffee.

"Now all we have to do is figure out who killed Branimir," Keely said. She tried to find a comfortable sitting position but couldn't. "Could we walk?"

Lane picked up his coffee. "Good idea." He followed her past the dessert display, the tables, and the landscape photographs for sale. The original wood floors announced the progress of their steps through the café and to the front door.

Outside, Keely rolled her shoulders back, closed her eyes, and felt the sun's warm hands. "Which way?"

"Left. There's a great house over here." Lane led the way.

"Do you think Stockwell detonated the second bomb?" Keely asked.

"Hard to tell. The only thing I know for sure is that Stockwell always looks out for himself first. Everyone else runs a distant second. If he says he didn't detonate the second bomb, he may be telling the truth, or he may be trying to avoid a longer jail sentence." Lane gradually increased his pace to keep up with his partner.

"Where do we look?" Keely asked.

"I've been thinking about retracing our steps and asking

for DNA from Zacki Branimir. But first, I think we need to talk with Mladen. From now on, we don't tell anyone when we're coming to have a chat. For now, at least, I don't think we should call in our location to dispatch. We can let Lori know, but that's about it." Lane stepped onto the curb and waited for a gap in traffic so they could cross Nineteenth Street.

"You don't think Stockwell acted on his own, then?" Keely looked left while Lane looked right. They stepped into the crosswalk.

"No. On the other hand, it's pretty clear that other members of the Scotch drinkers' club will be distancing themselves from Stockwell. Any association with Stockwell is beginning to look like a career-limiting move. Whoever tipped Stockwell to our location and your personal information isn't likely to come forward. The only way we'll know is if Stockwell tells us who it was. Chief Simpson will put the communications department under a microscope. So we should be safer now." Lane pointed at a house on their left. It was a two-storey with rounded windows, a brick face, and copper pillars. The front yard consisted of wild flowers and Colorado blue spruce trees behind an ornamental iron fence.

"Nice." Keely smiled when she saw various toys scattered across the front deck. "Looks a little out of my price range."

"I just like looking. I get the feeling it's a happy place to live."

They continued walking.

"Let's go and see Mladen," Lane said. "I'd like to ask him a few more questions."

Fifteen minutes later, they walked into a camera and framing shop on Eleventh Avenue at the western edge of downtown.

Inside, they took in the pictures placed up near the top of the walls. "Someone's been to Greece." Keely looked at the photographs of the people and the houses climbing up from the seashore to the top of the hill.

Lane spotted the young woman at the counter and walked toward her. "Is Mladen in?"

She looked up from the computer screen, tucked her brown hair behind her ear, and said, "He should be upstairs." She walked out from behind the counter. Lane and Keely followed her up three stairs to a room filled with sample frames, a variety of borders, and a workbench the size of a pool table. She pushed open a door labeled EMPLOYEES ONLY. "Mladen! A couple of customers are here to see you."

The young woman turned, smiled, and walked past the detectives. "Thanks," Keely said.

The door swung open and Mladen appeared carrying a rectangular piece of glass. He looked at the detectives and gently set the glass down on the bench.

"We'd like you to look at some pictures." Lane placed a brown envelope on top of the glass.

Mladen looked at the envelope as if it might burn him if he touched it. He reached out to it then pulled his hand away.

Keely said, "They're pictures of some soldiers. We'd like to know if you can identify them."

Mladen's hand reached for the envelope, then pulled back again. He shook his head. "You don't know what this can do to me."

"What do you mean?" Lane asked.

"You don't know what you're asking. It's Goran, isn't it? I still have nightmares about the war. They're getting bad again." Mladen's face was white as he stared at the envelope.

Lane went to pull the envelope away.

"Wait," Mladen said. He took a long breath, picked up the envelope, and slid the photos out. He set all three on the bench. "The man is Borislav Goran. Both pictures are the same man. He is older in this one." Mladen pointed at the driver's licence photo. "He was the leader of the Tarantulas. He ordered the killings and the rapes." Mladen pulled over a stool and sat down. His eyes never left the photos. "The woman is older in this photo, but it looks like his girlfriend. She was a sniper. She guarded us while the Tarantulas took the men into the forest and executed them. All of the members of Goran's paramilitary unit had the same insignia on their jackets. Some of them even had tattoos up here on their shoulders." Mladen touched the shoulder of his right arm. "Yes, that looks like her."

"A name?" Keely's voice was just audible.

Mladen shook his head before looking at the detectives. "We never knew her name." He pointed at Keely and the vivid bruise on her face. "You were injured in that explosion? The newspaper said two detectives were injured."

Keely nodded. "Yes, it was us."

Mladen looked at Lane. "Do you think you know what war is like?"

"No," Lane said.

"The militia—these Tarantulas—they took a coffee break after the killings, before they started the rapes." He pointed at the picture of Jelena. "The woman watched. She smoked her cigarettes and she watched. The Tarantulas joked about what they were going to do to us." Mladen looked at the detectives in turn. "I hope that you will never find out what war is like."

"Where were you on Sunday morning at ten o'clock?" Lane asked.

"Leo and I were at Prince's Island. It was a busy day for us." Mladen took the photos, put them back in the envelope, and handed them to Lane. "After the explosion, are you still the same people?"

After a few years on this job, I'm a different person.

"The flashbacks happen all the time," Keely said.

Mladen showed them his thumb and forefinger, holding them barely a millimetre apart. "You've had a tiny taste of what war is like."

"Why are you so kind to the children in your performances?" Lane asked.

Mladen hesitated, as if suspecting a trap. "My mother made me promise not to become a killer. To become a man who was kind to children. A man she could be proud of."

"Do you have a cellphone?" Lane asked.

"Of course. You want the number?" Mladen recited it. Lane wrote it down. As he turned, he saw Mladen spraying the worktable with cleaner and wiping at the spot where the photos had been. *I wish it were that easy to wipe away a memory.*

A few minutes later, Keely opened the passenger door and got into the Chev. "Let's go have a chat with Leo."

Lane drove north, then east to a computer store up the hill from the centre of the city. They parked next to a camouflage green and grey SUV the size of a bus.

"Either somebody's trying to make a statement or has a bit of a Napoleon complex." Keely undid her seat belt and watched a middle-aged woman climb into the SUV and put on her glasses.

"Or it's somebody's mom on a shopping trip." Lane smiled as he looked over the roof of the Chev.

Keely shook her head. "Smartass." She covered her mouth when she realized what she'd said. Lane laughed and walked to the computer store.

Inside, a receptionist sat at the head of a line of desks. Behind her sat a row of five salesmen. No one looked up.

Keely and Lane stood in front of the bespectacled receptionist. She looked up and blinked at them through magnified eyes. "Yes?"

"We'd like to talk with Leo, please." Keely showed the receptionist her ID.

"I'm in here." Leo's head popped up from behind a monitor. "I'll be right out."

The secretary stared at her computer screen and said,

"He'll be right with you."

Lane looked around. Software and hardware were neatly stacked along the walls and shelves. Three customers were playing with demo computers.

Leo said, "We can meet in here." He held his right hand up and guided them through a glass door into an office, and closed the door. "Sit down."

Lane and Keely looked at one chair behind a desk and another in front of it.

"I'd prefer to stand," Keely said.

"Mladen said you two were nearly blown up in that explosion on the weekend." Leo leaned on his crutch with his back to the glass door. "He phoned about ten minutes ago, and I thought the two of you might show up here. You're here to see if we were working downtown on Sunday morning and we were." Leo turned to look through the glass at his co-workers. "All the people I work with know so much about computers and so little about people."

"Did you see anyone in the crowd who could verify your story?" Lane asked.

Leo looked at him. "Don't know any names, but there are a few regulars who show up most Sundays." He smiled. "You could always come next Sunday and check."

×

"Dr. Weaver? It's Detective Lane." Lane sat in the Chev outside a café on Kensington Drive. Keely listened to Lane's end of the conversation from behind the wheel.

"I just wanted to confirm that there's a viable DNA sample from the remains of Andelko Borimir." Lane waited and smiled at Keely. "Thank you. Oh? Sure. No problem." Lane looked at the phone and pressed END. He looked at Keely. "Next time we drive by that café in Parkdale, he wants us to pick him up some more Nanaimo bars."

"Will they be able to get DNA from the remains?" Keely asked.

"He thinks so."

"Good. Let's get a coffee and go visit Jelena." Keely pulled the keys out of the ignition, checked her hair in the mirror, and eased out of the car.

×

Lane threw his paper cup in a garbage can two doors down from Jelena's Alterations. Keely followed. Lane opened the door of the shop and looked inside. Three women were working at their sewing machines. Jelena wasn't one of them.

"I'm here."

The voice came from the parking lot. Jelena smoked a cigarette. She stood between a pickup truck and a van. She dropped the smoke. It rolled under the truck. "What you want?"

"A DNA sample to confirm that the remains we found are Andelko Branimir," Keely said.

"From me? Go ahead." Jelena moved closer.

"From your daughter. From Zarafeta," Lane said.

"Go fuck yourself." Jelena walked past them and into her shop. Not one of the women working on the sewing machines raised her head.

After they got back in the car, Keely said, "We need this. We need to prove that Andelko didn't leave Calgary, and that he is the father of Zacki. That way we've got solid proof about the identity of the body. Otherwise, anyone could argue that we have only circumstantial evidence and Branimir really did go back to his old hometown."

"Getting admissible evidence may be problematic," Lane said.

"One way or another, we need to know we're on the right track."

"It's not going to be easy." Lane pulled on his seat belt.

"You're forgetting something. I've never met the daughter."

Lane looked at Jelena's shop. He looked at Keely. "I wonder if any of the condominiums in that complex are up for sale?"

×

Lori looked up from her desk as Lane and Keely walked into the office. She gently hugged each of them in turn. "How come you're here? You should be off work for at least a week."

Lane refrained from stretching the sore muscles that were complaining after Lori's hug. "We have a couple of things to do."

Lori looked at Keely. "Don't you be thinking that just because the big boy is back, you have to be back too."

Keely said, "Whoever made that bomb tried to blow both of us up."

"I thought you got the asshole — oh, sorry — the *suspect*." Lori leaned back against the desk. "By the way, word's getting around to the members of the Scotch drinkers' club that they'd better lay off. Suddenly, the members' list for the club has dropped down to one or two. People who were regular members are saying they only went to keep an eye on Smoke. Others are saying they only went to have a drink or two and talk with their friends. It's all become very innocent. And nobody else is buying it." Lori cocked her head in the direction of Gregory's office. "Notice how he's making himself scarce?"

We need to solve this case, not worry about Smoke and his buddies. "We need to get a DNA sample and we need your help. We also need to find out if your friend at The Hague can get any other photos of the woman in Borislav Goran's militia unit."

Keely looked at Lane. "Have you got the listing?"

Lane smiled. "We need to see if it's possible to put a residence under surveillance." He pulled a piece of paper from his pocket and handed it to Lori. "It's for sale and it's across the street from the Branimir residence."

"How about a couple of real estate agents having an open house?" Lori asked.

"The kitchen overlooks Jelena's home," Keely said.

"I know just the pair for that job. I'll get a call in right away." Lori reached into her drawer. "And if I hurry, I might just catch our friend in The Hague." She held up a business card. "He's right here."

×

Matt came upstairs to find Lane putting a leash on Roz. "Where are you going?" Matt yawned.

"Roz and I are thinking about taking a run down by the river." Lane rubbed the dog behind the ears and stood up.

"Mind if I come along?" Matt went into the kitchen and filled a glass of water.

"Not at all." Lane waited at the front door.

Christine came upstairs. "Where you goin'?"

"Down by the river to take Roz for a walk." Matt stuck his feet into his running shoes.

"Can we come?" Christine asked.

"Sure," Lane said.

"Daniel! Wanna go for a walk?" Christine yelled down the stairs.

Arthur's eyes opened. "What?" He sat up on the couch.

"We didn't want to wake you after you had all of those tests today," Matt said.

"I'm coming too," Arthur said.

The six of them sat cheek to cheek in the Jeep. Roz had the back of the cabin to herself and licked Christine behind the ear.

"Hey!" Christine wiped at her ear. Arthur turned to see what was up. Matt looked at Daniel, who was blushing. Christine laughed. "It was Roz!"

It took twenty minutes to reach the soccer fields on the flats between the river, the football fields, and the Trans-Canada Highway.

Lane parked on the gravel on the west side of the fields. The sun drew a shadow line halfway up the Douglas firs. The trees wrapped their roots into the steep, towering bank on the south side of the river.

Daniel and Christine squeezed out of the Jeep. "Which way are we going?" Daniel asked.

"Just wait." Matt lifted the rear door and put a leash on Roz. He walked toward the pathway heading east while Arthur, Christine, and Daniel looked west at the sky with its oranges and pinks. The sound of the river was soothing background music to Roz's panting, their footsteps, and intermittent conversation.

"Look at all the birds." Christine pointed north.

The soccer field was dotted with the blacks, whites, and greys of Canada geese foraging on the grass. A pair of birds flared their wings, honked, and whistled overhead. Lane watched them land.

Matt jabbed him in the ribs with an elbow. "Ready?"

"You bet." Lane walked off the path and onto the grass.

"What are you doing?" Daniel asked.

Matt bent to free Roz from the leash. "Sit." She reluctantly agreed while she whimpered.

"Ready?" Lane asked.

"For what?" Daniel looked at Matt and Roz.

"Spread out," Matt said.

"Cool." Daniel looked at the hundreds of birds in the field. Matt began to skip to the right. Lane ambled to the left. Matt was gaining momentum. "Run!"

Roz accelerated. "I'm not running!" Arthur walked.

Lane ran toward a tight gathering of birds. A few had their beaks tucked under their wings. The setting sun made all of the colours richer. Lane inhaled the cooling mountain air. He looked ahead. The geese were running, flapping their wings, and a few rose into the air. Lane looked to his right. The birds were a wave of motion alongside of him.

Arthur began to run.

Lane was in among the birds now. On his left, he was eye to eye with a goose whose wingspan matched the detective's height. On his right, a smaller bird was honking at ear level.

Christine cried out. Lane smiled at the pure joy in her voice. The birds rose above their heads. Daniel screamed with exhilaration. Lane stopped, open-mouthed, to look up. The cloud of undulating, honking bodies began to turn toward the city centre.

Someone ran into Lane. Lane's jaw snapped shut on his tongue. He tripped and fell.

Arthur tumbled onto the grass beside Lane.

Daniel handed Lane a glass full of ice. Lane lifted the glass in thanks and slipped a cube into his mouth. He winced as the ice touched his bruised and swollen tongue.

Matt came upstairs. "Your clothes are in the wash."

Christine took a bag of ice, wrapped it in a towel, and laid it gently on Arthur's ankle, propped on two pillows at one end of the couch. Three pillows at the other end cushioned his head. "Owwww," he said. "Thanks."

Lane closed his eyes and smiled at the memory of all those birds rising into an orange sky.

"Ewwww!" Christine backed away from Arthur.

"What?" Arthur turned his head.

"I'll get you a tissue."

"What?" Arthur waved his hands in confusion.

"You've got goose shit in your ear!"

chapter 16

Lane stared at Keely, who had her hair down and wore jeans, red shoes, and a black T-shirt. She looked five years younger and decidedly unhappy with what she was wearing. Lori was frowning. *They're going to try to drag me into a discussion about clothes so that I won't think about Arthur and tomorrow's operation*, Lane thought.

Keely frowned. "How much do you want to bet I end up following Zacki into a mall?"

Lane looked at Lori for support. She glared back. "Don't look at me and don't say anything, because anything you say could and should be held against you." Lori pointed a pencil at him as if she were about to stab it into his eyeball.

"You both look great," Lane said. *Hurry, change the subject.*

Lori pointed her pencil in the air. "He's learning."

"Have you heard from our man in The Hague?" Lane mumbled.

Lori let the tip of her pencil point at the desktop. "You'll be the first to know. What happened to your voice?"

"He bit his tongue." Keely sat in the chair across from Lori's desk.

Lori focused on Keely. "I smell a story."

"He was chasing geese. Arthur ran into him. Lane had his mouth open."

Don't even try to explain, it'll only make it worse.

"Arthur sprained his ankle, Lane bit his tongue, and they both got covered in goose *droppings*." Keely covered her mouth in mock horror.

"No shit?" Lori fluttered her eyelashes. "Couldn't you and

Arthur spring for a room somewhere?"

"Time to go to work." Lane picked up his jacket and waited for Keely.

"I'll drive." She put her hand out for the keys. He gave them to her.

"Good," Lane said. "This time we have a full-size pickup."

Inside the truck, Keely was all business. "The observation team is set. They have our cell numbers. Should we wait at the golf course? I figure it's the least likely place for either Jelena or her daughter to go."

"Sounds good."

After the thirty-five-minute drive, Keely went into a coffee shop while Lane waited inside the truck. Then they drove to the parking lot of the private golf course across the street from Jelena's condo complex. The detectives parked under a tree to drink their coffees and watch the luxury cars carry members to and from the club.

Lane looked at his watch. "It's eight o'clock. How long do you think we'll have to wait?"

"She's what, fourteen??

Lane nodded. Keely laughed. "If she's up by noon, we'll be lucky."

Keely was off by fifteen minutes. At 11:45, Lane's phone rang.

"Thank god—if I have to look at anymore golfers practising their swings in the parking lot, I'll have to shoot one of them. All those guys at the Scotch drinkers' club were golfers." Keely sat up and started the engine.

Lane listened to the officer on the phone. "The subject is on foot and headed south."

Keely pulled out of the parking lot and drove one kilometre to the main road, then turned south. They spotted Zacki walking along the sidewalk running along the east side of the roadway. Keely drove past her and into the parking lot where a bank, supermarket, pizza joint, and gas station were situated at each of the four corners of the mall. They parked next to a van. Lane watched the girl through a pair of binoculars.

"She always wears black?" Keely asked.

"Not sure." Lane watched as Zacki walked in the front door of the gas bar and walked out three minutes later with a red plastic fuel container. An attendant followed her, filled the container, and took a bill from Zacki. She waited until he returned with the change.

"What does she need that for?" Keely asked.

"I'm guessing diesel fuel and fertilizer."

"So?" Keely started the engine.

"Mix the two together, insert a detonator, and you've got an explosive device." Lane watched as Zacki switched the container into her left hand and struggled up the sidewalk. "This will take a while."

"How do you know so much about explosives?" Keely asked.

"Spent a summer with my cousins on my uncle's farm in Saskatchewan. They mixed diesel fuel and high-nitrogen fertilizer and used it to blast a hole in the ground so they could make a cold room to store vegetables."

"And they say Muslims are terrorists. Sounds like your family had its own cell in Saskatchewan. Do you think that maybe the Branimirs have a lawnmower?"

"Those run on gasoline. Besides, they live in a condo complex. Someone is hired to cut the grass."

They watched Zacki walk up the hill, stop, set the fuel down, switch hands, and continue walking. It took her ten minutes to reach the gap in the fence she used as a shortcut to get back to her home.

"Maybe we should head back to the golf course," Keely said.

Lane's phone rang. "Yes?"

Keely tried to hear the other end of the conversation.

"Good, we'll wait here." Lane turned to Keely. "She put the fuel in the garage, then headed out again. She's. . ." He looked through the field glasses. Zacki appeared through the gap in the fence. ". . .coming our way."

About three minutes later, Zacki turned the corner across from the service station and waited at the bus stop. She reached into her pocket and began to talk on a cellphone.

"Here comes the bus," Keely said.

The bus stopped. As it pulled away, Keely turned on the engine and followed it down Crowchild Trail, then accelerated to reach the train station ahead of Zacki.

"I've got my phone." Keely pulled up at the train station, put the truck in park, picked up her purse, and got out. She glanced at Lane.

"I'll be right behind you." Lane slid over behind the wheel. He watched Keely as she walked across the bridge and down to the platform level. Three cars of the C train pulled up. Lane drove to the exit and waited at the lights. He put his phone on the seat next to him. When the light turned green, he turned left and followed the train as it rolled down the centre of Crowchild Trail.

Lane's cell rang. He watched the road as he flipped it open. Keely's voice was on the other end. "Oh. Hello. Yes, I'm on my way downtown." She stopped talking for a full ten seconds as if she were listening to another person speak. "Yes. I'm meeting a friend." She waited. "I'll phone you back after we get off." She hung up.

Okay, so now we're watching Zacki and a friend.

When they got off the train downtown at City Hall, Lane saw that Zacki's friend was wearing blue. She was a head taller than Zacki, and her hair was blonde.

He watched them walk north toward the river, followed by Keely, as the lunch crowd walked the opposite way toward various office buildings. The girls talked nonstop, walking side by side, oblivious to anyone else trying to navigate the sidewalk. They came to an intersection and stepped into the crosswalk. Tires squealed, a horn blared, and the blonde girl yelled at the driver.

Keely waited for the light while the girls entered a hobby store occupying a two-storey sandstone building stuck between two office towers. From beneath the eaves, gargoyles looked down on passersby.

The driver behind Lane honked. Lane maneuvered the truck into an alleyway and parked.

Five minutes later, Zacki and her friend walked out of the hobby store, each carrying a bag. They jaywalked across the street and ducked into a coffee shop. Keely crossed the street inside a crowd of pedestrians, walked south to the coffee shop, and went inside.

Lane stood beside the front fender of the truck, watching and waiting.

Forty-five minutes later, Zacki and her friend walked out of the shop with their bags and headed toward City Hall.

Lane got into the truck. His phone rang. "It's Keely. I thought those two would never stop talking. Can you pick me up? We've got a DNA sample for Fibre."

Lane closed the phone, started the truck, and turned north onto Centre Street. Keely jaywalked and climbed in when he pulled up to the curb. She held a paper bag. "Got her DNA on this cup. You can always count on teens to forget to clear their table."

Lane waited while she put on her seat belt.

"All I had to do was sit there and drink coffee. It was like her friend was hooked up to a microphone. She talked so loud and asked so many questions." Keely sat up straight. "Can we stop soon?"

"Too much coffee?" Lane asked.

Keely's face turned red. "There's a restaurant at the top of the hill. Dylan and I go there. I'll show you."

She must have had more than a few cups of coffee. She's talking a thousand words a minute. "What did the friend say?"

"She asked about the stuff they bought at the hobby store. Apparently it's fuel for RC models."

"RC meaning remote control?"

"I think so. Then Zacki began to talk about how weird her mom was. Zacki explained about having to buy diesel fuel this morning. Jelena just started planning a trip yesterday, out of the blue. So the two of them are going to the passport office later on today or tomorrow." Keely crossed her legs.

"Almost there."

"How long does it take to get a passport?" Keely asked.

"At least three days, I think."

Keely held on as Lane turned left and pulled up to the curb. She handed him the bag. "Hold this."

She left the van, slamming the door shut behind her, and ran up the sidewalk into a Vietnamese restaurant. Lane's phone rang. He opened it. "Hello?"

"It's Lori. Stockwell wants to talk. Apparently he's being very insistent. How soon can you get back here?"

Lane looked at the bag with the sample. "Ninety minutes?"

"I'll let them know." Lori hung up.

Stockwell probably wants a deal. But what is he offering?

Keely opened the passenger door. "Thanks."

"Stockwell wants to talk," Lane said.

"So?"

Lane frowned. "We'll see if he'll say anything else of interest." He shoulder-checked and pulled out. "But we need to get that DNA sample to Fibre first."

Twenty minutes later, Lane drove past the turnoff to the hospital. "You missed the turn!" Keely cried out.

"It'll only take a minute to pick up some Nanaimo bars for

Fibre." Lane looked at his partner and raised his eyebrows. "I'm betting it will save us time in the long run."

"We need a rush on the sample, and the treat will get things moving along?"

"Exactly."

"I think I'm getting the hang of this." Keely smiled.

They found Fibre folding his lunch bag, wiping the crumbs off his desk into his palm.

"We have a favour to ask." Lane held the sample in his hand.

"And a treat." Keely held up the Nanaimo bars.

"Bribery?" Fibre asked.

"Yes, and we have a reason. Our suspects may be getting ready to leave the country. We need a comparison with Andelko Branimir's DNA." Lane put the evidence on Fibre's desk.

"Then it's a priority." Fibre stood up, wiped the crumbs off his hands as he leaned over the garbage can, and picked up the sample. "I'll take those." He grabbed the Nanaimo bars from Keely. "It might take as long as a month for the lab to get us the results." Fibre smiled at them and was gone.

The door closed. Lane laughed. "A lot of good that's going to do us."

Keely nodded. "We'll have to find some other way."

It took forty minutes to drive back downtown and find the interrogation room where Stockwell waited with Roper, his lawyer. Lane and Keely went into a nearby room and watched the pair on the monitor.

"Where's the union rep?" Keely asked.

"Perhaps the Scotch drinkers' club is culling Stockwell from the herd." Lane looked at Keely. "Is Buck here?"

"There they are." Keely pointed at the TV.

Buck and Lesley walked into the interrogation room. "Sorry to keep you waiting," Buck said. He turned as another person entered. "This is Brad Williams, the crown prosecutor."

Williams nodded and crossed his hands at his belt. He wore a suit, a frown, and about two hundred pounds on a football player's frame. Roper nodded back.

"You wanted to talk with us?" Buck sat down across from Stockwell, who was wearing sweats and a T-shirt.

"I've got some information that will help you." Stockwell looked at the camera. "I can testify that you were set up by Smoke when he initiated the investigation into the missing Glock. That getting Harper to investigate you was a calculated move to discredit both of you." Stockwell looked at his lawyer.

Roper said, "In exchange for my client's testimony on your behalf, he will serve no jail time."

Williams pointed at Stockwell. "You set off an explosive device. You are going to jail."

"I didn't have anything to do with the second bomb!" Stockwell's face turned white. "I can't go to prison." He rubbed his forehead with the open palm of his right hand.

The imagination can be a wonderful motivator, Lane thought as Buck let the silence stretch out, like maple syrup on snow.

Stockwell stared at the wall. "I can prove where I was the morning the second bomb went off. And I was there in the room when Smoke thought up the plan to have you investigated. Gregory was there too."

"That still doesn't prove you had nothing to do with the construction of the second bomb. Besides, the second bomb was detonated with a cellphone. You didn't have to be there." Williams shook his head.

"I'll plead guilty to sending the letters, making the calls, painting the garage door, and making the first pipe bomb, but I had nothing to do with the second bomb. I don't know who did that." Stockwell looked at Buck.

Buck never mentioned the graffiti on the garage door.

"In order to detonate the second bomb at the right time," Roper said, "the bomber would have had to be close by. My client was one hundred kilometres away. We have witnesses."

Buck looked at Roper. "Have you got a card?"

Roper fished a business card from his pocket. Buck took it. "I'll get back to you."

×

"What is RC fuel used for?" Lane thought aloud. He and Keely sat in their office with the door closed.

"You don't think Stockwell tried to kill us?" Keely sat next to Lane behind her desk.

"No. At least, my gut tells me that. And the fact that he admitted to painting your garage door. That wasn't mentioned in the first interview. The problem is, we need more evidence to back that up."

"He was just trying to scare me?" Keely hesitated for a moment. "And he's not capable of being a killer?"

"He's definitely capable. I've seen him kill. But if he was going to kill you, why not kill you with the first bomb? All he had to do was wait for you to get into the car." Lane checked the interdepartmental phone list on the computer. He reached for his cellphone. "I want to check one thing." He dialed. "Yes. It's Detective Lane. I have a question about explosives." He waited. He covered the mouthpiece and raised his eyebrows. "I'm on hold."

Lori came to the door and handed a folder to Keely. "From The Hague." Keely opened the folder.

Lane took his hand away from the phone. "I have a question about the fuel used to power remote control models. Does it act like diesel fuel when mixed with fertilizer that's high in nitrogen?"

Keely read the information from the folder.

Lane hung up. "That fuel Zacki bought yesterday at the hobby shop."

Keely looked up. "Yes."

"Bigger bang. The explosives expert thinks that RC fuel was used in the second bomb. He said it's more powerful than diesel fuel mixed with fertilizer." Lane looked at the folder. "What have you got?"

"There's very little information on the woman who fought with the Tarantulas, but there is another picture." Keely handed it over to Lane.

He studied the photo. Men holding automatic rifles and wearing combat fatigues posed around the front of a tank. A man and a woman sat on the turret . Lane looked at Keely.

"The girl sure looks a lot like Zacki," Keely said as she flipped through a second document. "And it says here that the remains of Andelko Branimir were found in a mass grave a month ago."

"So Goran stole Branimir's identity?" Lane asked.

Keely nodded. "Definitely a possibility."

"We need to talk with Mladen." Lane stood up and tapped his pocket to make sure he had the truck keys.

"Do we need to show him this picture?"

"Yes."

"We'd better hurry. You've got an appointment, remember?" After that, Keely was quiet until she aimed the pickup down Eleventh Avenue. "Harper said this would happen."

"What did Harper say?"

"He said at some point you'd start to figure it all out. You'd put all of the pieces together, and I should watch how you do it." Keely pulled the seat belt away from her chest.

"Harper told you that?"

"Of course. He told Simpson that you and I should work together. Let me in on what you're thinking, will you?"

"If Stockwell didn't detonate the last bomb, and if Mladen isn't involved, then we'd better be very careful with Jelena. She's getting her daughter to stock up on fuel." He looked at his watch. "If Jelena is buying fertilizer and components for a detonator on the way home from work, we're in trouble. She's obviously had some military training and appears to have the survival instincts."

Keely looked at the dresses in the windows of several bridal shops along Eleventh Avenue. "So how do you do this?"

"Do what?"

Keely shoulder-checked. "Put it all together."

"Information. Gather as much of it as possible, then. . ." Lane looked ahead without seeing the traffic.

"Then?" Keely asked.

"It comes together."

"Very scientific." Keely looked out the windshield. "Jelena is very protective of her daughter."

"Yes."

"Mothers can get pretty ferocious when it comes to protecting their children."

There was no parking in front of the photo shop where Mladen worked, so Keely pulled into the alley at the back.

Mladen was sitting in a lawn chair with his eyes closed. He held a can of pop. He opened his eyes when the detectives opened the doors of their truck.

"Coffee break?" Keely asked.

Mladen nodded. He sat up straighter.

"Would you look at another picture for us?" Lane asked.

"Tarantulas?" Mladen's voice was filled with what sounded like inevitability.

Keely offered the picture. Mladen took it, but waited before examining it. When he finally looked back at the detectives, it was as if he had aged a decade.

"The girl in the picture?" Lane asked.

"She was the one with Goran. A sniper. The Tarantulas killed up close. She killed from a distance." He handed the picture to Keely.

"How old was she at the time?" Lane asked.

Mladen shrugged. "Sixteen, seventeen."

"Can you remember anything else about her? Anything she said?" Lane asked.

Mladen looked down the alley, into the past. "'It is war.' While she kept her rifle aimed at us, she kept saying, 'It is war.' It was if she was saying that we should accept what was happening to us, because we were in a war and someone else had control over life and death. That it was the war which was responsible, not her."

"Would you be able to identify her if we asked?" Keely slipped the picture back into a manila envelope.

Mladen nodded.

Lane handed him a card. "If you remember anything else, please call."

Mladen took the card and stared at the detective. Lane began to leave, then turned back to Mladen. "When's your next performance?"

What might have been a smile under different circumstances appeared on Mladen's lips. "Saturday. Eau Claire."

×

Dr. Alexandre sat with her hands in her lap. She crossed her left leg over her right and smoothed the crease in her red slacks. "Who was the person who told you that you don't deserve to live?"

The doctor's question hit Lane with a combination of surprise and shock. *Delay!* Lane thought. "Do you mean who said those exact words?"

Alexandre waited for an answer.

"My mother."

"How old were you?" The doctor picked up her coffee and drank.

Lane was struck by the casual tension. "Thirteen, I think." *How did Alexandre suspect?*

The doctor's tone remained relentlessly calm. "And since then?"

"As recently as a week or two. My sister-in-law alluded to it." Lane set his cup down, put his feet flat on the floor, and measured the distance to the door. He put his hands on the arm of the chair.

"When was your first suicide attempt?"

Lane glared at the doctor. *What the hell?* "I was nineteen."

"Describe the circumstances, please." Alexandre leaned a centimetre or two to her left and placed her elbow on the arm of the chair.

"I was driving down a hill. There was a bridge at the bottom. I accelerated and aimed the car at one of the bridge supports. Then I turned away."

"And after that?"

"I planned it out once or twice but never got that close again."

The doctor shook her head. "I think you're not being totally honest with me."

"Who gives a shit what you think?" Lane stood up, half out of surprise at his reaction and half out of a desire to flee.

"Sit down."

Lane sat.

"Your job involves observing human behaviour and drawing conclusions. Now *your* behaviours are being observed." The doctor uncrossed her legs and leaned forward. "When you saved Cameron Harper's life, there was a man behind the door who was threatening you with a hunting rifle."

"That's correct." Lane heard his voice as if someone else was doing the talking. *She can't be right!*

"And after that, you were wounded once."

"Yes, but that was completely accidental."

The doctor shook her head. "And you went back on the job even though you were told to take time off. Then you put yourself in harm's way again."

"Yes."

"How did it feel when you found the child in the garbage can?"

You brutal bitch! He wiped the sweat away from his forehead and felt a cold trickle of perspiration rolling along his ribs. "Shocked. Guilty."

"Guilty?"

Lane smiled. "I was still alive. She was dead. She was a child — an innocent."

"Are you beginning to get the picture?" Alexandre's eyes continued to stare at Lane, analyzing his reactions.

Lane felt his throat constrict. His eyes filled with tears. The other part of his mind remained detached, as if observing his own reactions. Then emotion took hold and savagely shook him. He began to sob.

Dr. Alexandre spoke in a voice that was resigned and firm. "You couldn't kill yourself, so you took risks. You tried to run down a suspect, and a truck hit you. Then you were punished for rescuing a girl of kindergarten age. Maybe it's time you began to listen to the people who wish you well."

Lane looked out the window. *Like Arthur, Matt, Christine, Keely, Harper, and Lori?*

"It may be time to make some changes."

"Run with the geese." Lane spoke without thinking. It felt like someone else was saying the words.

"Explain." Dr. Alexandre sat back in her chair.

Lane told her about Matt's prescription for depression.

"I think we need to book a family session," she said.

chapter 17

They watched Arthur follow the operating nurse down a polished floor. He wore a blue housecoat and slippers. They waited until the automatic doors closed behind him.

Lane turned.

"Where are you going?" Christine asked.

"*We*," Lane said.

"We?" Matt asked.

Lane pulled his cellphone out of his pocket. "The surgeon will call after the operation. We're going to get something to eat. It will be a long day."

Matt and Christine caught up to him and walked on either side. They stayed in that formation to the elevator, down to the main floor, and outside to the car.

Matt drove while Lane studied the neighbourhood of Parkdale as they passed the open schoolyard, the new houses being built, old ones being renovated, and cyclists funneling onto the river pathways. He reached into his pocket several times to ensure his phone was on.

Matt pulled in front of the café. "They open?" he asked.

Lane glanced at his phone to check the time. He looked at the café. An OPEN sign was in the window. He opened his door. "Wait here." Lane walked up the steps to the café and went inside. The tables were empty. No one was behind the counter. He heard the door open behind him. He turned. Christine waved.

Matt looked around at the oak tables, the desserts be-hind glass, and the cash register. Christine moved to the left and looked through a half-open door into the kitchen.

Lane followed and looked over her shoulder.

A waiter sat in an office chair, straddled by the cook, still wearing her hairnet. They were both blonde and in their mid-twenties. The cook had a butterfly tattoo on her ankle.

The wheels on the chair began to squeak.

"Oh!" Christine backed away. Lane did the same.

"Oh my God," said the cook.

"I love you, baby," said the waiter.

Lane and Christine retreated to a booth around the corner, where Matt sat with a newspaper, open to the comics page.

"What's going on?" Matt asked.

"A little nooky in the kitchen," Christine said.

"I hope they wash their hands before they prepare our food," Lane said. Matt appeared not to be listening.

The waiter arrived behind the counter two minutes later. He was a little short of breath. "Sorry, folks, I'm Jim. Didn't see you come in. Come on up and I'll take your orders." The group stood and approached the counter.

Matt said, "Come on baby, light my fire!"

"Sorry?" asked the waiter.

Christine elbowed Matt in the ribs. "Mochaccino for me," Matt said, rubbing his side. Christine ordered the same.

"Make it three, please," said Lane, "and we'd like some sandwiches."

"A threesome?" Matt asked. Christine punched his shoulder.

The waiter blushed as he pointed at the order forms and multicoloured highlighters for ordering sandwiches. Lane picked up three forms and passed them out.

"Would you like a side order of nooky with your pickle?" Matt asked Christine. She glared at him while standing on his foot.

The waiter brought them their coffees and they sat back down. Matt sipped his mug quietly. Christine sat next to him, careful to keep him within elbow range.

Soon after their soup and sandwiches arrived, an older man with an enormous mustache entered the café and strode over to their table. "How's the service?" he asked.

"Very good, thank you," Lane said.

Christine tried to kick Matt under the table.

"Ouch!" Lane exclaimed, rubbing his shin.

Matt laughed. The waiter chuckled. Soon, Christine joined in as well.

Lane's laughter started slowly, but he was roaring by the time a group of joggers arrived at the café, dressed in their sweats and skin-tight shirts and drenched in perspiration. They glared in the direction of the laughter.

The waiter turned to the mustached man. "Sorry, Fred," he said. Fred shook his head and moved behind the till, then into the kitchen.

Matt laughed louder.

The waiter caught his breath. "Thanks for not squealing on me to my boss."

"You knew?" Christine said.

"It's hard to miss clues like 'Come on baby, light my fire.'" The waiter's face turned red.

"What fire?" Lane asked.

"Exactly," the waiter said. "Dessert's on me."

Two hours later, Lane was sitting on a bench with Christine while Matt skipped rocks across the Bow River. His phone rang. He flipped it open. "Hello?"

"Dr. Dugay here. The operation went well. We got the tumour. There was no evidence that the cancer spread into the sentinel node. Of course, the node and tumour will be sent to the lab for a biopsy. The results normally take a week. Arthur will come out of the anesthetic within the next hour and will be assigned a room from there."

"How soon can we see him?" Lane asked.

Christine faced her uncle. Matt looked up from the edge of the water.

"Phone this number in an hour," the surgeon said.

Lane checked his sticky note and compared it to the number on his phone's call display. "Thank you." He closed the phone and looked at Matt and Christine. "He came through the operation just fine. We call back in an hour."

"Let's go," Christine said.

"Where?" Lane asked.

Christine rolled her eyes.

"To get him some flowers," Matt said.

Arthur was asleep and propped up in bed when they saw him an hour later. A pair of plastic tubes on either side of his chest drained fluid into plastic bottles. There were bandages where his breasts used to be.

The man in the next bed looked to be over eighty. He was trying to pull his IV out.

Arthur continued to snore.

Lane checked the time. "I'll stay if you want to go home," he told Christine and Matt.

"I want to be here when he wakes," Matt said. Christine nodded in agreement.

"He's sleeping," Lane said. "I'll stay with him. You two take a break and get a coffee." He handed them a couple of bills. "Bring me back a coffee too, please."

Arthur woke up ten minutes later, recognized Lane, and asked for some ice. Lane fed him a couple of cubes. Arthur chewed the ice while he tried to focus his eyes.

"Dugay thinks he got it all," Lane said. "He thinks it didn't spread."

Arthur tried to smile, but pain forced his mouth into a grimace instead.

"What do you need?" Lane asked.

"Where are the kids?"

"I asked them to go get coffee. I wanted to ask you something."

"Well?" Arthur looked at the ceiling.

"Do you still love me?"

chapter 18

"Dr. Weaver asked you to call." Lori sipped her morning tea.

Lane pulled his cell out of his pocket and flipped it open. It was dead. "I need to put this on the charger," he muttered. He walked to his office and plugged his phone in. He reached for the phone by the computer and dialed Fibre's number.

"Hello?" Fibre was eating some kind of root vegetable. His voice was barely audible over the sound of chewing.

Lane held the phone away from his ear. "It's Lane returning your call."

"I tried to phone your office number, as requested."

Lane heard the annoyance in Fibre's voice and ignored it. "You have the results for Branimir?"

"Not yet." Fibre swallowed.

"How long will it take?"

"It may take longer than a month to determine if Andelko Branimir is the father of Zarafeta Branimir. My initial estimate was incorrect."

"That complicates things," Lane said.

"Unavoidable." Fibre hung up.

Lane got up, walked out of his office, and found Keely talking with Lori. "Morning."

"What's new?" Keely asked.

Lane waited by the fax machine. It began to whir. "We'll have to wait for DNA results."

"How long?"

"Up to a month," Lane said.

"So what do we have to talk with Jelena about?" Keely asked.

"We'll have to think of a new approach."

"What about Stockwell? He still wants to talk about making a deal to keep his ass out of jail." Keely read the fax over Lane's shoulder.

"Stockwell will have to wait."

"He could testify on your behalf. He could prove that Smoke abused his position to smear you." Keely put her fists on her hips.

"It has to wait. The Branimir case is at a critical stage."

"And there has been an organized attempt to ruin your career." Keely stood between Lori's desk and the wall, effectively blocking his escape.

What has got you so riled up? "And we have a fourteen-year-old in the middle of a situation that is extremely dangerous. Which one of these situations deserves priority?"

Keely leaned against the wall. "We deal with Jelena first."

"Yes."

"What about Arthur?" Lori asked. Her phone rang. She picked it up. "He's right here." Lori covered the mouthpiece. "It's one of the guys keeping an eye on the Branimir home."

Lane reached for the phone. "Lane here." He listened. "And the daughter hasn't returned?" Lane nodded and looked at Keely. "The mother is inside?" He nodded. "All right, call me on my cell if there's a change. We're on our way." He hung up and looked at Lori. "Thanks."

He turned to relay the message to Keely. "Jelena took Zacki out early this morning. Zacki carried a gym bag. About an hour later, Jelena returned without her daughter. There haven't been any signs of movement from Jelena since." It was Lane's turn to put his fists on his hips.

Keely waved the fax. "We're going to have a heart-to-heart with Jelena?"

Lane nodded. "I need to get my phone."

In ten minutes they were exiting downtown in a non-descript Chevrolet. Lane looked out over the river as Keely drove west. Three inflatable rafts floated by. The people inside leaned back and chatted. One rafter reached into a cooler and passed around cans of beer.

"What do we say to her?" Keely asked.

"We tell her we have evidence that proves her husband was Borislav Goran, a war criminal. Then we show her the picture of the Tarantulas and comment on how much the woman looks like Zacki. We'll see where the conversation goes from there." Lane looked ahead as Keely took the ramp onto Crowchild Trail.

"What about the bomb-making ingredients?" Keely eased into traffic.

Lane looked down onto the river and at the city centre beyond. "I'd like to work that in with our talk about Zacki. The last time I mentioned Zacki, Jelena got angry. We'll see if she gets angry, then I'll slip in the question about the explosives."

Ten minutes later, Lane's phone rang. "Lane."

Keely could hear the voice of the officer but not the message.

Lane flipped his phone closed. "Jelena just drove away from her home. The car is loaded down, and she's wearing fatigues. One of the officers is staying behind to keep an eye on her condo. The other is following her." Lane flipped his phone open and checked the battery. "How's your phone?"

Keely pulled her phone out and handed it to Lane. He checked the battery. "Yours is good. Mine's low."

Three minutes later, Lane's phone rang. He listened, looked at Keely, and pointed straight ahead. "Speed it up. She's headed toward us from the opposite direction."

Keely accelerated. "Lights and siren?"

"Not yet." Lane closed his phone.

Keely stopped at a set of lights near the western edge of the city. Earthmovers were creating a mound of dirt in preparation for bridge construction.

"There." Lane pointed at a white car turning south. The words JELENA'S ALTERATIONS were painted on the driver-side door. Lane saw Jelena's face and was sure she had spotted them.

Keely turned the lights on, pulled out, and waited for traffic to stop. She turned left. The engine roared as she turned off the lights and raced to catch up.

"Leave the lights on," Lane said. "She's already spotted us."

Lane listened to the radio as the officer in the other car called for assistance. He picked up the radio. "The suspect may be armed and is wanted for questioning in a roadside bombing. Approach with extreme caution. Alert the bomb unit."

"Shit!" Keely said. They were stuck behind a pair of minivans driving side by side, ignoring the siren and the lights flashing in their mirrors. Ahead of them, Jelena drove across the bridge spanning the railway tracks and river, flanked by a stand of towering Douglas firs. When Jelena passed the concrete barrier on the other end of the bridge, her car skidded as she braked. She turned right off the pavement, bounced over the curb, and onto the grass.

Lane spoke into the radio. "The suspect has left the road on the southwest side of the Stoney Trail Bridge. We need to block access on the north and south ends of the bridge. Do you have confirmation that the bomb unit is on its way?"

Keely braked. The bruises on Lane's chest muscles screamed as the seat belt tightened against his body. Keely inhaled sharply as the belt gripped her ribs. She left the pavement and aimed the Chev down into the ditch.

Lane saw Jelena's car nose into the trees. Both front doors were open. "Stay back from her car!"

Keely stopped. Dust boiled up around the Chev. Lane saw Jelena at the edge of the Douglas firs. The trees stepped down to the river two hundred metres below. Jelena carried a duffel bag over her shoulder. She reached inside her fatigues as she stood behind the trunk of a tree.

Lane undid his seat belt. "Down!" he shouted, grabbing Keely by the shoulder, pulling her toward him. Her head banged against his shoulder. Lane caught a glimpse of Jelena's hand coming out and around the trunk of the tree, holding a black object. He ducked behind the dashboard. He felt Keely brace herself and did the same.

The concussion from the explosion hit them a millisecond before the blast of heat.

Tricked by the proximity of the explosive concussion, the airbags deployed, shoving the detectives against their seat backs.

The airbags deflated. Debris rained down: smaller projectiles at first, then larger chunks of metal and plastic.

Lane peered over the dash. Nothing remained of Jelena's car but four wheel rims and an engine. The rest was blackened bits of wreckage. A door lay between the wreck and the Chev. The roof was lodged near the top of one of the trees. Flames licked up a Douglas fir on the left.

Lane picked up the radio while Keely surveyed the damage. "We need fire, rescue, and the tactical team at the southern end of the Stoney Trail Bridge. A car bomb has been detonated. The suspect is being pursued on foot. She is headed west."

Lane dropped the radio on the floor. He looked at Keely. Her eyes were wide. She touched her right hip to see if her Glock was still there. Lane checked for his weapon. Keely pushed her door open.

Lane looked toward the trees as he got out. *Man, I'm glad I can hear the traffic noise*, he thought, noting the sound of cars accelerating as they reached the first of the series of foothills rolling up to the feet of the Rocky Mountains. He glanced at Keely. "Your ears okay?"

She nodded and took a step forward.

"You stay here with the car," Lane said.

Keely shook her head. "We both go. Just tell me where you need me."

There's no time to argue. "Let me get to the trees. You stay behind the Chev and provide cover. Once I'm there, I'll wave you on and cover you."

Lane drew his Glock, walked along the bottom of the ditch, then up the side and into the trees. He walked past the garage door opener Jelena had used to detonate the car bomb. He looked downhill and caught a glimpse of her traversing the hill, making her way deeper into the forest. He turned to Keely and crouched, pointing his weapon in Jelena's direction to cover his partner's progress.

When he felt her hand on his shoulder, he pulled out his cellphone. "Put yours on vibrate and my number on speed dial. One buzz means Jelena is in sight. Two means one of us is in communication with her." Lane set his phone to vibrate.

Keely flipped her phone open and manipulated the settings. Lane pointed to the left. "You take the high ground. I'll go down toward the river. Watch where you put your feet in case she took the time to set booby traps. Remember, Mladen said she only kills from a distance."

"And remember, she's protecting Zacki," Keely said. "That makes her especially unpredictable."

"Point taken." Lane moved down the slope at an angle intended to close the distance between him and Jelena. After fifty metres, he crossed a paved trail zigzagging its way down the slope. The sound of sirens and the scent of smoke sifted through the trees.

Lane looked over his shoulder and caught a glimpse of

Keely working her way from tree trunk to tree trunk about thirty metres above him.

Continuing to angle his way down, Lane holstered his weapon and used his hands to slow his descent until he could hear and see the river loping lazily east. He spotted a gravel trail and a set of stairs below. He reached the trail and eased under the railing. *She'll be expecting this. But she can't watch Keely and me at the same time. And why blow up the car? It makes it almost impossible for her to get away. It's like she wants us to hunt her down.*

He kept his right index finger alongside the Glock's trigger guard.

Jelena wants us to hunt her down and to protect Zacki.

Lane followed the trail. He looked down through a gap in the trees to the river. The water was turquoise. It turned into diamonds as the sun rose higher. He listened for sirens and traffic. Instead, he heard crows squawking, the river running, and his footsteps on the gravel.

He looked ahead and above. A fallen tree trunk was wedged in against three standing trees. It offered perfect cover. Lane kept his eyes on it as he worked his way along the trail.

The sound of a motorboat broke the silence. Lane looked down. The fire department's riverboat left a white water wake as it sped upstream. There were three men in the boat. One looked back and up at Lane. Then the boat was gone.

Lane looked up the path. A preschooler ran toward him. Behind the boy came his smaller brother and his mother with an infant tucked against her breast. The father trailed them.

Lane holstered his Glock.

"Elias! Wait for us!" the mother said.

Elias was a blur of curly blond hair. He stopped, smiled at Lane, and ran past. The smaller boy ran after Elias.

"Sorry about that," the mother said as she forced Lane to the outside edge of the path.

"Hello," Lane said to the father. The man smiled back. "When you get to the end of the path, you'll be met by police officers. Tell them what you saw. Now please get your family out of here." Lane pulled his Glock out and regretted the terror that lit the father's eyes.

He pushed past the detective. "Elias! Finn!" The man ran down the trail.

Lane scanned the trees and brush above and below him. On the downslope side of the trail, he spotted a one-metre retaining wall pressed up against a tree trunk.

He smelled a cigarette.

He looked above the trail and saw Jelena sitting cross-legged on the near side of a tree. She was smoking, a rifle cradled in her lap.

Lane held his arms away from his sides. *She isn't aiming the rifle at you so don't initiate any action.* The phone in his pocket vibrated once.

"Andelko was getting better, you know. At least he was much better before. . ." Jelena stubbed out the cigarette on the sole of her boot, pulled a pack of smokes out of her breast pocket, and lit another one.

"Before?" Lane asked.

"Before he saw the juggler." Jelena inhaled deeply.

"Then he started to drink again?"

Jelena pointed at Lane with her cigarette. "We both wanted to leave the war behind. To start over. But war never leaves you. Andelko would drink to forget, but how could any of us forget what happened in the war?"

"I don't know."

"That night. That night after he saw the juggler. Andelko came home and started to drink again. Then he came after me. This time I fought back." She looked past Lane to the river.

"You killed him?" *She has the advantage here. She must have spotted me before I saw her. What is she waiting for? She should have kept moving west. She knows how to disappear. But she can't without leaving her daughter as a suspect. Jelena has left us a trail to lead us away from Zacki.*

"I killed him. I dumped the body in the water by the road. I thought no one would ever find him. But this summer was so hot."

"And dry."

"Yes." Jelena smiled. "Very dry."

Lane heard the honking of geese. He saw Jelena's attention shift. He looked over his shoulder. A pair of geese travelled downstream. He saw their backs and their wings as they flew below him.

His phone began to vibrate. It stopped, then began again. It stopped and vibrated again.

It must be Keely. He reached into his pocket and flipped it open. "Hello?"

"Hey, uncle, it's Christine. Uncle Arthur is acting funny. They've got him on some kind of painkillers."

"Can I call you back?" Lane asked.

"You don't have time to talk to me?" Christine asked. "What could be more important than Uncle Arthur?"

"I can't talk right now. I'll call you back." Lane pressed END. He looked back at Jelena.

She leaned her back against the tree trunk. "It's beautiful here. Like home."

"You joined the Tarantulas?" *Keep her talking.*

"You think it was a choice? It was a necessity."

"How is that?" Lane glanced to his right, checking for cover in case Jelena aimed her rifle.

"It was war. I had no choice. If I wanted to survive, I had to join them."

She sounds like she's still trying to convince herself. "So you were at the village. You saw what the Tarantulas did?"

"Yes, I saw."

"Does Zacki know?"

"My daughter knows nothing!" Jelena lifted her rifle by the barrel so that she could lean on it when she stood.

A flash of insight struck Lane. *She wants me to shoot her! Then we have our killer and Zacki is free of it all!*

Jelena extinguished her cigarette against the tree trunk. "The others are coming."

"I don't hear them."

Jelena looked east. "I do." She stepped away from the trunk of the tree.

The rest was a series of impressions.

Jelena lifted her rifle, pointed it at the sky, and pulled back the bolt.

Lane lifted his Glock.

Jelena pitched forward, off-balance.

She rolled down the hill.

Keely slid down the slope behind Jelena.

The rifle cartwheeled down the slope. Lane stepped to his left as it spun past him.

He looked to his right as Jelena rolled onto the path. Keely landed on top of the sniper.

He ran forward.

Jelena grabbed for Keely's hair.

Keely had a canister in her hand. She sprayed Jelena in the face with pepper spray.

Jelena screamed.

Keely rolled Jelena onto her belly.

With her knee against her spine, Keely pulled one of Jelena's arms behind her back.

Keely's hair was filled with leaves and twigs. She tossed Lane the pepper spray. "Your handcuffs, please? I seem to have lost mine."

He handed her his cuffs, then covered Jelena with his gun while Keely fastened her wrists.

They sat Jelena up on the path. Her tears washed away some of the pepper spray. "What did you do to me, you Muslim bitch?"

Lane said, "She messed up your plan."

Jelena looked up at him. She tried to focus through her tears. "What are you talking about?"

"You were waiting for us to kill you." Lane leaned over to pick up Jelena's backpack. He looked down the slope where the rifle lay against the base of a tree.

Jelena shook her head. "I need a smoke. It would have been better for you to kill me."

Lane looked at Keely. "I need your phone."

She handed it to him, then brushed the debris from her hair. A trickle of blood leaked from the stitches along her forehead.

Lane dialed the phone. "Harper? It's me. We've got the suspect. Saliba disarmed her. We're coming out. Can you advise the tactical team?" He listened. "That's right, I trust you. I don't trust Smoke's good ol' boys." Lane flipped the phone closed and handed it back to Keely.

He stepped off the trail, skidded down the slope, and returned a few minutes later with the rifle slung over his shoulder.

"Let's go." Lane took Jelena by her elbow and helped her up.

Keely walked ahead.

They stopped halfway to light a cigarette for Jelena. She walked and smoked with the cigarette between her teeth. When they arrived at the end of the trail in the shade of the bridge, tactical officers stepped out from behind cover. Keely, Lane, and Jelena waited alongside the river.

Lane looked left. The river swirled around a bridge support. Traffic hummed over the bridge fifty metres above them. Lane spotted Staff Sergeant McTavish. *Good,* he thought.

Lane looked at Keely and moved his head to the right. They walked toward McTavish.

The Staff Sergeant smiled at Lane's approach. "In the middle of the action again, I see."

Lane chuckled. "Have you met Detective Saliba?"

McTavish shook Keely's hand. "Pleasure."

Lane looked beyond to the paramedics parked by the bridge support. "Ms. Branimir needs medical attention. Pepper spray and a few abrasions."

McTavish turned and waved. "We need the paramedics." He turned back to Lane. "The deputy chief gave me specific instructions. You hand the suspect into my custody. After that, he expects you in his office as soon as possible. A blue and white is waiting for you at the end of the trail." McTavish pointed to a trail winding its way through a stand of evergreens. He took Jelena by the arm and handed her over to a pair of black-clad officers. "Do either of you need medical attention?"

Keely looked at Lane and shook her head. McTavish pointed at her bloody scalp.

A member of the bomb squad reached for Jelena's backpack. Lane handed it over to him, along with the rifle.

The detectives walked past the officers standing alone and in pairs. No words passed between them. Lane and Saliba looked ahead toward the clearing. As they left the stand of evergreens, Keely asked, "You really think she was trying to commit suicide?"

"Absolutely. She set off a bomb to attract our attention, then waited for us to catch up."

"I still don't see how. . ." Keely brushed a burr off her shoulder.

"She made a point of explaining how she killed her husband. But first, last night, she took her daughter somewhere safe. It's all very calculated. A diversionary tactic to protect someone else." Lane inhaled the scent of the evergreen trees as he and Keely walked from shade to sunlight and back into shade.

"So she was protecting Zacki." Keely looked ahead and saw the blue and white parked next to a dumpster. The driver was leaning against the fender. The constable stood up straight as she recognized the detectives. She handed the keys to Lane, then opened the passenger door.

Ten minutes later, they were close to the Trans-Canada Highway when Keely asked, "How many bombs did Jelena make?"

Lane glanced at his partner in the rear-view mirror. "The one she used on us and the one at the bridge."

"Could we be missing one? Remember, Zacki bought diesel fuel first and then went to the hobby shop."

"Give me the radio," Lane said. The constable handed him the mic. "Dispatch? This is Detective Lane. I need immediate and direct communication with Staff Sergeant McTavish."

Lane waited a full thirty seconds.

"McTavish here."

"It's Lane. There is a high probability of another explosive device. Probably located at Jelena Goran's home." Lane gave McTavish the address.

"Understood," McTavish said.

Lane turned left off Sixteenth Avenue. "Where are you going?" Keely asked.

"To visit Arthur." Lane smiled.

"You sure the deputy chief won't mind?"

"If he does, I'll have a talk with his wife."

Within five minutes they were exiting the elevator on the tenth floor of the Foothills Medical Centre.

They found Arthur sitting up and dozing. Matt was leaning against the wall. Christine was in a chair across from the bed. She glared at Lane.

Lane asked, "How's he doing?"

Christine shook her head. "They gave him something to help him sleep. Something for the pain." She looked at Keely. "You're bleeding."

"Some kind of painkiller," Matt said.

"It's nothing," Keely said.

Arthur opened his eyes. "What's for lunch?" He spotted Lane. "Did you bring me a sandwich?"

Lane looked at Keely. She shrugged.

Arthur swung his legs around to get out of bed.

"We had to stop him once already." Matt leaned away from the wall.

"The lady serving lunch was pretty mad," Christine said.

"The guy next door has a better lunch," Arthur said with a smile.

"Better stop him, Uncle Lane," Christine said.

Matt blocked the door. "He'll steal another lunch if you don't."

"If I promise to bring you a sandwich from the café, will you stay in bed?" Lane asked.

Arthur sat back down, leaned his head against his pillow, and began to snore.

×

"What I don't understand is why she would want to blow up her house." Harper sat in his office with Lane and Keely.

"Destroy the past, I think. She probably didn't want her daughter to know about the Tarantulas. After the forensic team gets through with their search of the house, they'll probably uncover more proof that Andelko Branimir was Borislav Goran." Lane leaned against the arm of his chair. He looked at the pictures of Harper and his family on the wall.

"If she's killed and her house blows up," Keely said, "then all of our attention is focused on Jelena and away from her daughter. If you look at it that way, Jelena's actions make more sense. She's protecting the daughter. The logical conclusion, then, is that Zacki killed her father."

Lane and Harper looked at one another.

"How come you're meeting with us now?" Keely asked. "I mean, you told me you had to keep us at arm's length."

"Things changed this morning." Harper looked directly at Lane. "Stockwell still thinks if he can make a deal, he won't have to spend time in jail. The crown prosecutor says no deal."

Keely laughed.

"What's so funny?" Lane asked.

"Stockwell is such a stupid asshole. He still thinks he can get away with it."

"Well, for a long time he did," Lane said.

"You need to see this piece of evidence." Harper leaned over and pulled a photocopy from his desk.

"What is it?" Keely asked.

"A show of good faith by Stockwell. His lawyer had it delivered this morning." Harper handed it to her.

"What's it say?" Lane asked.

Keely said, "It's an email from Smoke asking Gregory and Stockwell to manufacture a charge against you to discredit you." She pointed at Lane. "It says, 'Manufacture anything short of a suspension. The objective is to force Detective Lane to resign.'"

"Remember how Smoke threatened you when we went after Dr. Jones?" Harper asked.

"Yes." Lane took the paper from Keely and read. "It even gives Gregory and Stockwell suggestions on who to tell that I'm under investigation so that word will get around."

"Chief Simpson told me to let you know that a formal letter absolving you of any and all charges is being drafted. The investigation of your conduct is concluded." Harper locked his fingers behind his head. "If you want to take legal action against Smoke, Gregory, and Stockwell, the door is wide open."

Lane shrugged. *The damage is already done.*

Keely's phone rang. She looked apologetically at Lane and Harper as she opened it. "Yes? Hi, Lori." Her eyes widened. "You're kidding." She closed the phone. "Zacki Branimir is downstairs waiting to talk with us."

"We have to go." Lane stood up and shook Harper's hand.

Harper's phone rang. He picked it up. "Yes?" He listened then held up his hand, indicating the detectives should wait. "No one was injured?" He listened. "Good." Harper hung up the phone. "You were right. There was an improvised explosive at Jelena's house. A grenade in an empty tin can was tied to the front door. It was rigged to fall out when the door opened. Underneath the can was a bucket filled with home-made explosive. The bomb disposal team is singing your praises for warning them before anyone went into the house."

When they walked into their offices five minutes later, Zacki was sipping a soft drink and sitting in the chair across from Lori.

Zacki stood up when she saw Lane. "What did you do with her? I can't find my mom."

Lane took her elbow. "Come on down to my office and we'll talk. I've seen your mom. She's safe."

"She is?" Zacki followed him.

"Lane! You sonuvabitch!"

Lane turned. Former Staff Sergeant Gregory stood at his office door with a cardboard box in his arms. His flesh was red right up to the top of his skull.

Keely faced the staff sergeant. "You backstabbing bastard. I remember you hitting on me at the Scotch drinkers' club. You asked me how much it would cost to put a smile on your face! Then you pointed at your crotch and asked me if I knew what a big treat you had waiting for me!"

Gregory turned white.

Lori stood up. "You said that to her? You've got a daughter

in high school! As far as I'm concerned, you deserve to be suspended!" She pointed at the door.

The door hit Gregory in the backside when the box jammed up against the doorframe.

The door shut.

It was as if all of the tension had been sucked out of the room. Lori smiled at Keely. "Nice work."

Lane looked at Lori and said, "Thank you for blowing the whistle on him and his buddy. One gutsy move on your part made a huge difference."

"You weren't supposed to know that!" Lori said. "I was told that it would be kept confidential. You detectives are so smug when you figure something out!"

"Thank you, Lori," Keely said. "Otherwise that bastard Stockwell would have gotten away with blowing up my car."

Lori looked sideways at the detectives. "Don't start thinking you're smarter than you are. Now get back to work."

Lane motioned for Zacki to come into his office. He waited for Keely to step inside, then shut the door. Zacki sat in the chair between the detectives' desks.

"Did you go home?" Lane asked.

"No. Mom told me not to go back when she left me at my friend's place. My mom's being all weird lately. Paranoid." Zacki wiped her eyes with the back of her sleeve.

"She was arrested this morning," Keely said.

Zacki looked at Keely and then Lane. "But she didn't kill my dad!"

Lane said, "Your mother confessed to killing him because he was drunk and beating her."

"Yes, he was drunk. Yes, he was beating her. He was punching her in the face. Then he started to choke her. I tried to pull him off, but he was too strong. So I hit him on the head with a frying pan. He fell on my mom. He wasn't breathing. That night we tied him to some blocks of cement.

We drove around until we found a place to dump the body. It was a pond or something. We were in mud up to our knees. My mom told everyone my father moved back home." Zacki began to sob. "I killed him."

×

"You look like you had a rough day, uncle." Matt sat at the foot of Arthur's bed. Christine sat next to him.

"Something like that." Lane smiled at the two of them.

"You were there, weren't you?" Christine looked sideways at Lane. Matt looked at Christine.

"Well?" Christine asked.

"Where?" Lane asked.

"Don't even try! When I called this morning, you were in the middle of it all." Christine shook her head.

"Yes, Keely and I were there."

"How close were you to the explosion?" Matt asked.

"Not that close." Lane braced himself for the second blast of the day.

"Was your vehicle damaged?" Matt asked.

"Slightly."

"Shithead," Christine said.

×

"Well?" Lori and Keely were waiting when Lane returned.

"Christine called me a shithead." Lane looked to Lori's right at Gregory's empty office.

"She figured out what happened today?" Lori asked.

Lane nodded.

"Sounds like she had every right to call you a shithead," Lori said.

Keely touched his shoulder. "When does Arthur get to go home?"

chapter 19

"Hello." Lane picked up the phone by the bed and looked at the time.

"I know it's early. I can't find my son."

Lane heard apology and worry in the woman's voice. "Who's your son?"

"Daniel. He didn't come home last night. I thought maybe he and Christine. . ."

Please don't finish that sentence. Lane sat on the edge of the bed. "I'll go check." He slipped on a pair of sweats and walked downstairs to the kitchen.

Roz got up and whined at the door.

After letting the dog out, Lane went down into the family room, where he found Daniel sleeping on the floor and Christine sprawled on the couch, snoring, with one leg on the floor.

Lane went back into the kitchen and picked up the phone. "He's here, asleep in the family room."

"Thank you! Please get him to call when he wakes up." She hung up.

Arthur lay on the couch in the living room. "Who was that?"

Lane walked out of the kitchen and into the living room. "Dan's mom. How are you feeling?" He looked at the plastic containers draining from Arthur's incisions and safety-pinned to the pockets of his pajamas. The containers were filling with a pinkish liquid.

"Tired."

"I need to change your dressings and empty those drains," Lane said.

chapter 20

Dr. Alexandre asked, "You were there when the car exploded at the bridge on Friday?"

Lane reached for his coffee. "That's right."

"And the suspect was armed?"

"Yes, I get your point," Lane said.

"You're still angry with me?" Dr. Alexandre was wearing white slacks and a white blouse today. As always, her collar was buttoned all the way to the top.

Lane took a long breath. "Yes."

"I see." Alexandre sat back in her chair and wrapped her hands around an oversized cup of coffee.

She really knows her coffee, Lane thought, inhaling the aroma.

"Well?" she asked.

"Of course I'm angry. You said I was trying to kill myself, that I was taking risks as a way of inviting self-destruction. My reaction was immediate and raw." Lane looked at the creamy coffee in his cup. "And it still feels like an open wound."

Alexandre waited.

"Still, when I looked back on the pattern of behaviour — *my* pattern of behaviour — I didn't come to the same conclusion that you did.

"Well?"

"I like the rush." Lane blushed.

"You like being shot at?" Alexandre seemed taken aback.

"I feel totally alive. When I'm on the hunt for a killer, it's the same. It's real, it's raw, it's very elemental. I feel like justice is possible when I'm after a killer. And when there are kids involved. . ."

Alexandre waited.

"I found a dead child in a garbage bag, and I saw another child's body in the back of a camper. Their parents murdered those children. I don't ever want to see that again. I feel sometimes, when I'm after the killer, there's a chance, a small chance, that a child can be saved."

"Have you managed to save a child?"

"Perhaps twice. Yes, I think we were in time twice."

"That's what drives you?"

Lane tried to smile, but he felt it turn into a grimace. "That and the smell."

"The smell?"

"The smell of death. It stays with me until I find the killer. I can't get rid of it until I see the killer in handcuffs."

Alexandre frowned.

"What?" Lane asked. *You don't believe me.*

"Where did you first smell death?"

"In the neighbour's backyard."

"What?"

"I was a kid."

"How old were you?"

Lane closed his eyes. "Five or six."

"Can you tell me more?"

"The neighbours had a daughter. She was fifteen or sixteen at the time. They said she was sick and couldn't go to school one winter. The next summer, I heard a baby crying. I even saw the daughter sitting with the baby at the kitchen table. Then there was no baby. A couple of weeks later, their dog was digging in the garden. The girl's brother chased after it with a shovel. And for a long time, until winter came, I could smell something in their backyard. I didn't smell it again until I found the little girl in the garbage can." Lane opened his eyes. "I always wondered what happened to that baby. Now I know."

"Did you mention it to your parents?"

Lane nodded. "I tried to tell my mother."

"What was her reaction?"

"She used a belt on me and told me never to speak to anyone about it again. You're the first person I've told since her."

chapter 21

"Roz needs a walk." Lane sipped coffee while he sat on the deck.

Roz's head lifted at the mention of the word "walk." Arthur dropped his chin, pretending, unconvincingly, to be asleep.

A car door closed. Roz lifted her head.

"What time do the kids get home?" Lane asked.

"Christine won't be back 'til six. She's driving the beer cart today. Matt should be back by noon." Arthur reached for his coffee. He winced with pain.

Roz barked. The doorbell rang. Lane got up. "I'll get it. Need a refill?"

"Please." Arthur handed Lane his cup.

Roz followed Lane into the house.

Arthur closed his eyes and felt the warmth of the sun on his face and arms. He heard muffled voices inside the house. He opened his eyes when the back door opened.

"Hello." Joseph stood in the doorway wearing a black golf shirt and casual grey pants.

"Go ahead and sit, I'll bring out some coffee." Lane looked at Arthur with an unreadable expression.

"It's nice back here." Joseph sat down and looked around at the variety of marigolds and gladiolas. He bent to pet Roz. She growled and backed away to get closer to Arthur. She crawled underneath his chair. The hair along her back stood up in a ridge.

Lane opened the back door, balancing a tray with three coffee cups, milk, and sugar. He set it down on the table.

"Where's Christine?" Joseph asked.

"At work." Lane caught a whiff of his brother's aftershave. *Smells like money.*

"Oh? Where?"

"A golf course." Lane bent down to pet and reassure Roz.

"Which one?"

"Lynx Ridge. Matt works there too." Lane watched his brother, who was avoiding eye contact. Lane fixed a fresh cup of coffee for Arthur and handed it to him.

Joseph stood to add sugar and cream to his coffee. He sipped. "Very good."

Lane waited for Arthur to take the first sip of his coffee, then got up and fixed his own.

"Are you the person with the green thumb?" Joseph asked Arthur.

"Yes. It gets me outside." Arthur studied Lane as he sat down.

"Very nice." Joseph nodded with approval at what he saw.

What do you want? "You were in the neighbourhood? On your way to a golf game?"

Joseph sipped his coffee and looked at Roz, who kept watch from under Lane's chair. "I thought perhaps we could reach an agreement over the will. There has been correspondence from your lawyer, a Mr. Thomas Pham."

"Tom is our lawyer." Lane looked at Arthur.

"It would be better if we settled this one like family." Lane noted the patronizing tone in his brother's voice.

Joseph looked at Arthur as if he expected him to get up and leave them alone.

"Arthur's my family. As are Matt and Christine." Lane felt the old rage clawing its way up his throat. *Use it! It'll keep your mind sharp!*

"Very well," Joseph replied, his voice dripping with disapproval.

You didn't think I would get a lawyer. You thought it was a bluff.

The realization almost made Lane smile. "What do you want?"

"I want to settle the will." Joseph met Lane's eyes and looked away.

"As I said before, we have two children to educate." Lane set his coffee down. *Before I throw it in his face! He'll do anything to keep this quiet, to keep it out of the papers. Joseph Lane's brother is gay!*

Joseph inhaled. He pulled a pen and two sheets of paper from his pocket. He slid one over to Lane. "You write down a figure that you think is fair, and I'll write down what I think is fair. Then we'll negotiate."

"We need a third piece of paper." Lane looked at Arthur.

Arthur shook his head. "It's okay," he told Lane. "You take care of it."

Joseph wrote down a figure and folded the paper in half.

Lane worked out the price of books and tuition in his head, then multiplied by two. Then he thought, *Fuck you!* He wrote down a number, added two zeroes, and showed it to Arthur, who blanched.

Joseph slid his number over to Lane and waited for Lane to do the same.

Lane opened his brother's piece of paper and looked at the figure. He worked the numbers in his head. *It'll cover school for Christine and Matt with some left over.*

"Your figure is a bit imaginative," Joseph said.

"Yours is a bit frugal." Lane folded the paper in half and folded it again. "Besides, my number includes Mr. Pham's expenses."

"A very generous fee." Joseph pretended to sip his coffee.

Lane waited and watched his brother. He could hear Arthur set his cup on the table.

Roz groaned.

Joseph tapped his close-cut manicured fingernails on the cup.

Lane closed his eyes. "Perhaps the best way to settle this is the way a family would. A bit of give and take. We add the two numbers and divide by two. Then I phone Thomas to get his approval." Lane opened his eyes.

Joseph rubbed his bottom lip with his thumb and forefinger. "Agreed. Thomas will contact me with the amount we've agreed on, then?" Joseph stood up.

"I don't foresee any complications." Lane remained seated. He watched his brother open the back door, enter the kitchen, and close the door behind him.

"Aren't you going to say goodbye to him?" Arthur asked.

"We did that a long time ago." Lane drank his coffee.

"How does it feel?" Arthur asked.

"How does what feel?"

Arthur looked at his coffee cup. "Being bought off."

chapter 22

"Explain," Lori said. "You look like shit."

Lane smiled. "You really do know how to cut through all of the crap, don't you?"

"At least you're smiling now." Lori looked at Keely. "She's got some good news."

Lane looked at his partner. "Well?"

"I went to talk with the ladies at Jelena's Alterations. They have this plan to keep the business going and take care of Zacki. She stayed at Rasima's place the other night." Keely crossed her arms.

"That *is* good news." Lane sat down.

"He's officially out of here." Lori hooked her thumb over her shoulder to indicate Gregory's office.

"And Stockwell is gone." Keely leaned against the wall.

"Smoke has his own reality cop show," Lane said.

"You've got to be kidding!" Lori stared open-mouthed at Lane.

"No way," Keely said.

"No, I'm kidding. He's just playing golf, networking, and enjoying his retirement." Lane shook his head.

"Sounds like being in hell. I hate golf," Keely said.

"I prefer quilting with the girls." Lori began to smile.

"What?" Lane asked.

Lori laughed. "I wonder if they sell Scotch at those fancy golf clubs?"

✕

"Thank you for being here." Dr. Alexandre wore a navy blue skirt and a pink blouse. She made sure that everyone had either coffee, tea, or water. Christine and Arthur sat on the couch. Lane and Matt sat across from them in chairs.

Christine asked, "Why did you want us to be here?"

Alexandre said, "I've got Lane's point of view. Now I'd like to see the big picture, the family picture. By the way, do any of you know his first name?"

"I don't know," Christine said.

"Don't ask me," Matt said.

"I promised not to tell," Arthur said.

"It's Paul," Lane said.

Matt shrugged.

Christine said, "What's so bad about that name?"

"St. Paul's words are often quoted to condemn people like me," Lane said.

"Oh," said Christine.

The doctor turned to Arthur. "How are you feeling?"

"A bit better every day. Waiting for the results of the biopsy."

Alexandre nodded at Arthur. "How is Lane doing?"

Arthur looked at Lane. "Better, I think. He saved a girl in kindergarten and her older sister. He was punished for solving the crime. It took its toll."

"Why is that?" Alexander asked.

"Smoke is an asshole," Christine said.

"He was punished for doing the right thing. He was punished for saving the little girl's life. He was punished for putting a killer in jail. He was punished for defusing a situation at Tsuu T'ina. Smoke even tried to take credit for the success of that operation." Arthur took a sip of tea.

"And Uncle Lane's been withdrawing from us," Christine said. "Pulling away. He gets angry all the time."

"He takes care of us," Matt said. "He takes care of all of us. I just think he's been really sad lately."

"Why do you think that is?" the doctor asked.

"The work," said Matt. "Our home life. Uncle Arthur's illness."

"You think it's me, don't you?" Christine said.

"No," said Matt. "I think it's us. We create a lot of stress for both of them."

"Actually, it's neither of you," Lane said.

"What is it, then?" Alexandre asked.

"I don't know how to put it into words yet."

chapter 23

"I'm going downtown to see the malabarista," Lane said to Arthur as Matt came in the door and kicked off his shoes. His heavy canvas pants were stained from the knees down with dirt and grass from working at the golf course. "Do you want to come?"

"Why?" Christine stepped into the kitchen.

"Why not?" Matt smiled. "Let's go."

"Can Daniel come?" Christine asked.

"Ask him," Lane said.

"Okay." Christine went to the top of the stairs. "Daniel? Come on!"

Arthur looked up from the papers he had strewn across the dining room table. "It's about time we got out of here. Summer's almost over." He let Lane get a jacket for him so he could hide the plastic tubes and drainage containers.

"I'll phone Keely," Lane said.

Twenty minutes later, they were jammed into the Jeep and driving along the valley bottom between condos, businesses, and skyscrapers.

"What's a malabarista?" Daniel asked.

"A juggler. In this case, it's two guys. One plays music and the other. . ." *How do I say what he does?*

"Juggles?" Christine asked.

"And does tricks," Lane said.

"You said he did some flips on stilts," Matt said.

"That too."

"That the guy with one leg?" Daniel asked.

"Yes," Lane said.

"So they play music, juggle, and do gymnastics," Arthur said.

"Just like the two of you." Matt laughed at his uncles. "Always juggling."

They parked just south of the river and west of the hotels and condos next to Eau Claire. A series of pathways met at Prince's Island, where walkers, joggers, cyclists, and babies in strollers funneled across a bridge over a pond. Ducks and geese fought for scraps and territory under the bridge and along the shore.

"Where will they be?" Christine asked as she took Daniel's hand.

"Just over by the water park, I think." Lane looked across the promenade, where parents were drying their children as they exited the paddling pool. Beyond the pool, older folks sat alone or together on the benches on either side of the promenade. A steady stream of people approached the bridge on their way to the park or the restaurant on the island.

The cheeky blast of a trumpet stopped feet and turned heads.

To those on the opposite side of the bridge, Mladen appeared to be walking atop the bridge's arch. Then he grew taller. In red and white, he glided over the bridge on stilts, swaying and twirling to the music. Now he appeared to be walking on the heads and shoulders of the people who looked in his direction. Leo followed behind, announcing their arrival. He played with one hand and maneuvered his crutch with the other. They moved in tandem — the malabarista and the musician — to the same tune.

On this side of the bridge, Mladen began to dance in a circle. The crowd backed away. Mladen balanced on his good leg. Leo picked up the beat, the trumpet accompanying Mladen's twirling.

The trumpet stopped. Mladen stopped too. His flowing

clothing swirled and caught up to him as he began to bounce on the spot then launched himself upward. At the top of the arc, he spread his arms, ducked his head, bent his knees, and flipped. He landed on his feet and completed another flip in the opposite direction.

Leo started up again with the trumpet. The crowd clapped.

"Amazing," Matt said.

Lane's phone rang. He opened it without taking his eyes from the performance.

"Lane? Look to your right."

He glanced east to see Dylan and Keely waving at him.

"Is this what you call an intangible?" Keely asked, then hung up.

Lane looked at Christine and Daniel, who held hands and watched the performance with frank admiration. Matt had his hand on Arthur's shoulder. Leo played a raunchy tune and they began to dance.

It doesn't get better than this.

ACKNOWLEDGMENTS

Bruce, for caring for us all these years — thank you.

Javi, thanks for the insights into a real malabarista.

Again, thanks to Tony Bidulka and Wayne Gunn.

Brad, John, and Bill, thanks for the legal knowledge and advice.

Bryce, Alex P, Mary, Alex K, and Sebi, thanks for the suggestions and feedback.

Nebal, thank you for the help with Arabic.

Karma, thank you for the Spanish translations.

Thank you to Crime Writers of Canada and their spirit of generosity.

Doug, Paul, Lou, Andrew, Natalie, Tiiu, and NJ, thanks for all that you do.

Thanks to creative writers at Nickle, Bowness, Lord Beaverbrook, Alternative, Forest Lawn, and Queen Elizabeth.

Sharon, Karma, Ben, Luke, Indiana, and Ella. What's next?

Garry Ryan was born and raised in Calgary, Alberta. He received a BEd and a diploma in Educational Psychology from the University of Calgary, and taught English and creative writing to junior high and high school students until he retired in 2009. That same year, Ryan received the Calgary Freedom of Expression Award in recognition of his outstanding contributions to the local arts community.

Ryan's debut Detective Lane novel, *Queen's Park* (2004), sprang from a desire to write a mystery that would highlight the unique spirit and diverse locations of his hometown. The follow-up, *The Lucky Elephant Restaurant* (2006), won the 2007 Lambda Literary Award for Best Gay Mystery. *A Hummingbird Dance* (2008) helped cement a loyal following for Ryan's books in North America and overseas. In 2011, the fourth Detective Lane novel, *Smoked,* was shortlisted for the Alberta Readers' Choice Award and nominated for the Lambda Literary Award for Best Gay Mystery.